Keepsake for Eagle Cove

a small town Oregon romance

by

M. L. Buchman

Discover more by this author at:
www.mlbuchman.com

Cover images:
Man And Woman Holding Hands Walking Photo ©
Geribody | Dreamstime.com
Douglas Fir Tree © Kongxinzhu | Dreamstime.com

Buchman Bookworks

Other works by M. L. Buchman:

Angelo's Hearth

Where Dreams are Born
Where Dreams Reside
Maria's Christmas Table
Where Dreams Unfold
Where Dreams Are Written

Eagle Cove

Return to Eagle Cove
Recipe for Eagle Cove
Longing for Eagle Cove
Keepsake for Eagle Cove

The Night Stalkers

MAIN FLIGHT
The Night Is Mine
I Own the Dawn
Wait Until Dark
Take Over at Midnight
Light Up the Night
Bring On the Dusk
By Break of Day
WHITE HOUSE HOLIDAY
Daniel's Christmas
Frank's Independence Day
Peter's Christmas
Zachary's Christmas
Roy's Independence Day
AND THE NAVY
Christmas at Steel Beach
Christmas at Peleliu Cove

5E

Target of the Heart
Target Lock on Love

Firehawks

MAIN FLIGHT
Pure Heat
Full Blaze
Hot Point
Flash of Fire
SMOKEJUMPERS
Wildfire at Dawn
Wildfire at Larch Creek
Wildfire on the Skagit

Delta Force

Target Engaged
Heart Strike

Deities Anonymous

Cookbook from Hell: Reheated
Saviors 101

Dead Chef Thrillers

Swap Out!
One Chef!
Two Chef!

SF/F Titles

Nara
Monk's Maze
The Me and Elsie Chronicles

Chapter 1

Envying other people wasn't something Tiffany Mills had much experience with and she didn't like it. Especially not when they were hugging her so fiercely.

She'd always thought of Natalya Lamont as the calm and collected one of her friends. Well, not her friends, but Natalya's. Maybe it was Natalya's own wedding that had her bubbling like a giddy schoolgirl.

Of course Natalya's mother also was exhibiting similar behavior as it was her wedding day as well—a mother-daughter marrying a father-son event. But Gina Lamont was a generally more effusive type, so at least it was expected of her.

Tiffany wanted to ask Natalya what it felt like to be so happy, but resisted the urge. Delaying a bride making the rounds wouldn't be fair…and, with Natalya's present mood, probably not even possible. It was awfully kind of her to notice Tiffany at all—she was as close to being a friend as Tiffany had allowed in years.

"I really appreciate you being here," Natalya finally let her go, then gave her another quick hug with a loud "Ooooooo" of sheer delight before spinning back into the congratulatory crowd surging through and around the Lamont B&B.

"No, it was my pleasure," Tiffany ended up saying it to herself, always remembering too late to speak her thoughts aloud when she was with others. If it meant she had lived too long alone, she wasn't going to think about it now.

It was a gorgeous day for spring in Eagle Cove, Oregon. The big Victorian overlooking the Pacific Ocean was packed with wedding revelers. The parlor and the kitchen overflowed out onto the porch on the warm May day. That was where Tiffany had retreated to, a small bench on the wrap-around verandah that let her overlook the events on the lawn without getting snarled up in them.

Becky Billings had lobbied to have the event out at her brewery, as her own wedding had been, and they would have moved it there if the weather hadn't cooperated. But it was one of those magical spring days after a long, wet winter that made everybody smile. Natalya and her mother Gina had thrown a lunch—catered by Greg, the town's master chef, of course—then had the wedding, which left plenty of time for dancing on the front lawn. It overlooked the ocean and was well filled with people during the warm afternoon; the cool evening would chase everyone inside, but not for a few hours yet.

Gina and Natalya had both wanted to be wed in the family home, the last house before the big headland that defined the end of Eagle Cove. The town was spread over two miles of shoreline and the town's founders—a mother and daughter as well—had built two grand Victorian houses on the high bluff below the rocky palisade of Orca Head. One house became the Lamont B&B, and Judge Slater owned the other.

Not for the first time, she felt a pinch. Gina and Natalya Lamont belonged here in Eagle Cove, direct descendants of the daughter. They even still lived in the family home, at least Gina did, and Natalya had grown up in it.

Tiffany was connected to the town as well, but it was a connection from long ago and one that she had kept secret for the three years since she'd moved here.

Of course she wasn't exactly in town, which made her feel a little less guilty. She lived alone, homesteading a full mile farther out of town into the forested hills. She had found a small gap between two plat surveys of adjacent state forests and, much to the Oregon Department of Forestry's surprise, had purchased the ten-acre anomaly from the state. She lived in "unincorporated" forest—technically, she wasn't even in a county.

Maybe she should declare her own county, or better yet her own country! Occupancy: one human, thirty chickens (unless some more eggs had hatched this morning), a half dozen goats, and her guard dog. There was also an exceptionally lazy cat the black-over-white color of an orca whale—and roughly the same blobbish shape—who kept Tiffany's lap warm on cold nights. Fitz only roused herself for mouse hunting, a task at which she excelled.

Oregon State law had some considerations that might make it implausible to declare independence and Federal law definitely did. Of course, if she did declare her own state, she'd have to decide whether or not to sign onto the Interstate Commerce Commission for fair trade with other states. Would that be necessary for when she sold her chicken eggs and excess garden produce to Greg at The Puffin restaurant in Eagle Cove? As a bonus she could elect a governor. Of course, with only one resident, the choice would be obvious and the balloting blessedly painless.

Tiffany raised her right hand, "And the ayes have it."

"Good. They can keep it," Jessica Baxter stepped up, slapped Tiffany's raised hand like a high-five, then eased herself down on the bench as close as Tiffany had observed best friends often did.

Tiffany's other shoulder was against a wall, so she had nowhere to go.

"If my husband ever tries to touch me again, he's going to get a big-ass *nay*."

"You're huge!" At eight months pregnant, Jessica seemed to be expanding daily, but she sat so close beside Tiffany, that Tiffany could see Jessica's belly almost from the owner's perspective. Jessica had been the first of Natalya's friends to get married. She'd gotten pregnant right away and every one of those eight months showed on her belly. She was five-ten—Tiffany wouldn't have minded those extra four inches herself—and slender as could be, except for the pregnancy. From the back she looked perfectly normal, as she had one of those pregnancies that went straight forward.

"Tell me something I *don't* know," Jessica groaned with a happy sigh of relief at being off her feet.

"Okay, you probably don't know why your five-times-great-grandmother stopped speaking to her daughter," for Jessica Baxter was Gina's niece and also a descendant of Pearl Lamont. And then Tiffany wished she could cut her tongue out. It was something Jessica wouldn't know, but it said so much more than Tiffany wanted to reveal. Ever.

Jessica blinked at her in surprise.

Tiffany could only hope that it would be written off as "just one of those things that Tiffany Mills says." Her own four-times-great-grandmother's journal was what had led her to Eagle Cove in the first place. Lillian Lamont had been one of the founders of the town. But if Tiffany wished to survive, her past had to stay hidden, cut off, forever.

"Wait." Jessica furrowed her brow as she massaged her back. "Five times…you're talking about the founders of Eagle Cove."

Tiffany really didn't do well with people who lived outside of her imagination.

Jessica, she knew, had been a journalist and was incredibly tenacious. Now that she'd latched onto it, there wasn't a chance that she'd let go. Tiffany didn't want to reveal how she knew what she did or that she had any connection to the town prior to the founding of the State of Tiffany in the woods. She suspected that her normal ploy of shaking her long hair forward and "going shy" while focusing on her knitting wasn't going to work this time. Especially as she hadn't brought her knitting to the wedding. Running might be an option. But if she started, she might never stop. Then where would she—

"Hi."

Tiffany looked up at the man now standing eye-level to them, two steps down from the porch. He was lean and had brown eyes beneath tousled hair of the same color. He wasn't dressed like a wedding guest, but rather in unseasonably early shorts, a plain t-shirt, and hiking boots. He looked like a trekker, certainly had the strong legs of one, but she glanced around and saw no sign of a pack.

"I don't want to crash the party, but I think I'm in the right place. This is the Lamont B&B?" He appeared a little lost and a lot overwhelmed, two feelings that Tiffany knew well.

Grabbing any distraction she could, Tiffany rose to face him as he climbed the last two steps. He was only a few inches taller than she was. "It is. It's also the Lamonts' weddings, both of them."

"Oh, that explains the crowd. Maybe I'll, uh, just come back in a few days." He looked around as if trying to find somewhere to go.

"Did you have a reservation?" Tiffany almost grabbed his arm as he started to turn away. Jessica hadn't moved from the porch seat close behind her and Tiffany was still trying to distract her from the accidental revelation.

"No. Not really. And not yet. I'm a couple days early. Once I got in my truck…" he waved vaguely back toward the long drive clogged with guests' cars, "I just drove."

"I think the B&B's full with wedding guests, but let's go check." Tiffany took his hand and led him inside. At the last second she risked a glance at Jessica, and saw that she hadn't gotten away with anything. But more than that, Jessica was looking at Tiffany as if she was suddenly an alien or something. She grabbed the man's hand more tightly and plunged into the crowd.

# # #

Devin Robison had rarely felt so out of place in his life. He'd slept in the back of his pickup last night in the Boise National Forest. Up with the sun, he'd landed in Eagle Cove nine hours later in the middle of a wedding. It was terribly disorienting, and not just the road-weariness-meets-wedding scenario.

He'd thought that growing up in Chicago had prepared him for great expanses of water. Lake Michigan was Chicago's front yard—three hundred miles long and a hundred wide. He'd even boated on the Caribbean a few times. But as he'd crossed the country, the towering peaks of the Rockies had been as disorienting as if he'd traveled to the moon. The real shock had been when he'd broken out of the Coast Range forest before the final descent into town and seen the entire Pacific Ocean before him; he'd nearly crashed his Toyota in surprise. Unless you happened to stumble on an island, Tokyo was five thousand miles away. The expanse was impossible to comprehend.

Neither Chicago nor the towns he'd driven through in the last four days had prepared him for the tiny size of Eagle Cove. One mile from forest to ocean and two miles along the beach…and it wasn't densely populated. The next town of any size was thirty miles up the coast. He'd been on the verge of turning around from an attack of agoraphobia, the fear of open spaces—or maybe just plain nerves. It was news to him that such obscure places even existed. Eagle Cove was so remote, so wild. He hadn't seen a single fast food place in the town. Maybe they weren't allowed; every business, actually every road except the main drag of Beach Way, had been named for a bird: Blackbird Bakery, Warbler Market, Rusty Pelican Tavern. Strange place.

Devin had come west looking for a fresh start, or at least a break. He needed the latter desperately, but he'd left "middle America" somewhere staggeringly far behind.

Finding the massive Victorian home had been easy. "Find LBB Lane at the far end of downtown," which was their grandiose term for a business district four blocks long. "Go to the end of the road Little Brown Bird Lane. You'll know when you find the right place."

And he absolutely had. The house was gorgeous. It was exactly the sort of structure that had led him into architecture school. Three stories of classic, early-1880s American Queen Anne Victorian. He'd fallen in love the moment he'd seen it. The house was one of the best examples he'd ever seen of that style. Unlike so many of the ones in Chicago, the whimsy had not been allowed to overwhelm the beautiful lines and overall cohesiveness of the design. Yet it was still playful, with circular turrets, balconies, and a wrap-around porch.

A verandah clogged with people.

Devin floated through a kitchen packed solid, anchored in this reality only by the hand of the woman leading him.

The woman leading him.

Few greeted her, though they readily moved aside, allowing her a straight line passage. His first sight of the kitchen had made him wonder if it was even possible to cross. Yet for whoever-she-was, the crowd made way. He was half tempted to guess that it was magic, as people almost didn't notice that they had moved aside for her. They certainly didn't break their conversations for her passage.

He usually at least knew the name of someone he was holding hands with. Had there been introductions? He didn't think so.

He'd headed for the woman on the verandah the moment he'd spotted her. Her nearly waist-long fall of thick tawny hair had acted like a guiding beacon. Only a model had hair like that, not normal people, yet she looked to be perfectly in her element. Then, as he climbed the steps, he'd become aware of her eyes watching him from beneath the wide brim of her felted hat—twin glints of blue-gray carefully hidden by shadow.

Her blouse and skirt were…rustic, for lack of a better word. Perhaps bohemian, as the maroon belt made by a wrapping of fabric defined a trim waist and made her billowy sun-yellow blouse and light spring-green skirt look very nice. Maybe someone's mild-mannered and carefully cloistered cousin.

Except for her hands. The one holding his was firm and, even if she didn't hold on hard, the strength of her fine fingers was obvious. And hard calluses. She worked with her hands a lot.

"What's your name?" She didn't look up at him. They'd come to a small nook in the back corner of the kitchen. It felt oddly quiet here though he could hear a dozen different conversations. She let go of his hand to pull out a register. The woman spoke softly, but he could hear her despite the other noise.

"Devin. Devin Robison."

She didn't offer her own, but began flipping through the pages. Then she stopped as if shocked. She looked up at him sidelong.

Yes, more gray than blue, at least the one eye inspecting him.

"Who are you?"

Devin figured that if he could answer that one, he wouldn't be twenty-three hundred and seventy-nine miles away from everything and everyone he knew. "Am I in the book?"

She nodded with a mesmerizing slide of long hair. "Yes."

"Is there a problem?"

This time the hair shimmered side to side.

"And?" What a curious person she was.

"Gina Lamont gave you the best room in the house other than her own. Until today it was her daughter Natalya's, though she's been living with her now-husband in town."

"I take it that's unusual."

She tipped her hat back enough that he could at least see a hint of a smile. "More than a little."

"Maybe we should check with her."

"Wedding day. I think she has enough distractions. Let me show you the way." She took a classic skeleton key from the hook and once again led him away, though without taking his hand this time. He kind of missed it.

Devin wanted to inspect the house as they went, but found himself unable to look away from the *still* nameless woman leading him up the twisting stairs and along a narrow hallway.

She knocked perfunctorily on the door and had the key inserted when someone called out, "It's open."

She eased open the door and peeked in.

"Tiffany!"

At least Devin now had a name for her. It fit. Fragile as glass in some ways, but enduring and undeniably beautiful. Also completely different from any woman he'd met before. The women in his Chicago social circle were consistently sharp, perfectly maintained, and elegantly attired.

A short blonde, dressed in a tight-fitting black dress with a dangerously bountiful cleavage, yanked the door wide and grabbed Tiffany by the wrist to haul her into the room, even though she was already retreating. Then the blonde, who seemed part small tornado, leaned around to look at him past Tiffany.

"Ooo. He's cute. Way to go, Tiff. Natya, check this out. We'll get out of your way, Tiff," she made the last lurid and suggestive.

The room was as classically Victorian as the house itself, high-ceilinged and it incorporated one of the circular towers as a small seating area. A white wedding dress lay spread across a dark quilt on the bed. Art covered the walls. Paintings and drawings of women. Powerful women.

Before he had a chance to notice more, a tall, dusky-skinned brunette spun to look at him. She too wore black. At a wedding? Above her left breast was pinned a corsage of tiny bud roses… spray-painted as black as her dress. Maybe some kind of joke? He was glad Tiffany instead wore the colors of spring; they looked very cheery on her compared to the other two women's, admittedly sexy, black.

The instant she spotted him, the brunette's expression went from surprise to narrow-eyed suspicion. She looked as if she'd leapt straight out of one of the paintings on the wall and was ten times more daunting in real life than the numerous two-dimensional women who seemed to be glaring at him also.

"No, I—" Tiffany was protesting as the blonde pulled her farther into the room.

It was easy to see what was going on and Devin was hard-pressed not to laugh.

The tall brunette stepped up close in front of him and his desire to laugh dissipated rapidly as he looked up at her. She stood at least five-ten and that was, he risked a glance to check, barefoot.

"If you so much as touch her, I'll personally—"

"No, Natalya," Tiffany cut her off. "He's a guest. I'm just showing him to his room."

The tall Natalya glanced over her shoulder, then she turned back to glare at him, her protective ire only slightly tempered.

"Hi, I'm Devin," he held out a hand. "I'm actually not a guest."

Natalya was halfway to shaking his hand, but stopped.

"A Gina Lamont hired me."

"Mom hired you?" The handshake never completed.

So the wedding dress had been Natalya's, Natalya Lamont's—Tiffany had said it was *both* Lamonts' weddings today. At a quick glance he saw that she and the cheery blonde both wore wedding rings. He double-checked, but Tiffany wore no jewelry. Neither rings nor earrings, at least not that showed through her hair.

"Well, isn't that convenient," the blonde said suggestively, winking at Tiffany, who blushed fiercely.

She fist-pumped at Tiffany's reaction.

"Yes! We'll be wearing black for you next. Another one bites the dust!" She began a small stomping dance, her bright red cowboy boots marking a muffled circle on the rich Oriental carpet.

Devin finally got the joke of wearing black—the "death" of another single woman.

Tiffany shook her head fiercely, creating a cloud of hair, but kept her peace.

Natalya's continued glare told him that her interrupted threat was still in place.

Devin felt as if he was suddenly swimming in deep waters. He'd come here for a fresh start, a reset on a life that had gone sideways (way the hell sideways), and he was already in it neck deep.

Welcome to Eagle Cove, buddy.

# # #

Tiffany slipped the key into Devin's hand and abandoned ship. She felt bad about doing that to him but she'd suddenly felt so claustrophobic, the room and the two strong personalities crushing in on her, that she had to run.

Downstairs was little better. The kitchen crowd surged into the parlor. Dance music sounded from out on the lawn. Danny McCall on vocals, the Judge (as everyone called the retired Judge Slater) on stand-up bass, and his wife playing a rocking lead acoustic guitar. Becky would be on the drums soon now that the music was gearing up. Tiffany played her harp with them on occasion, but not today.

Through the window, she could see that Jessica was still on the verandah bench. Tiffany didn't dare go out that door or she'd be trapped in a conversation she didn't know how to avoid.

She retrieved her harp from where she'd tucked it behind the basement door and made for the B&B's back door, ready to flee Eagle Cove just as her ancestor Lillian Lamont had over a century before…though Tiffany would only go as far as her farm, not all the way to San Francisco as Lillian had. Tiffany was *never* going back there.

Tiffany made it through the crowd, using the harp in its case as a shield, and opened the back door to escape just as Becky swept down the rear stairs. She hooked an arm through Tiffany's.

"Come on! They're waiting for us."

"There's no need…" Tiffany tried to point out that the band was already playing and people were already dancing on the lawn; therefore, no one was waiting for them, especially not for Tiffany. But she never had the chance.

Becky didn't let go, so Tiffany was helpless to head back to her home in the hills. Instead she was towed out the back door and around the house to where the band had set up under the spreading branches of a big old cherry tree on the front lawn. Becky deposited Tiffany on her usual seat, a nicely carved stump of a tree that had gone down in the Christmas Day Gale of 2005. She knew that because of the date carved by the chainsaw artist who had reshaped the stump.

At a loss for what else to do, she pulled her Celtic harp out of the padded case. The harp stood about three feet tall and had twenty-six strings, exceptional for a harp that she could carry on a shoulder strap and play while standing. As she was seated, she screwed in the lapbar crosspiece that would rest on her knees. The harp was one of her prized possessions, one of only two from her entire childhood—the only two she had brought north with her to Oregon and later to Eagle Cove. From the inlaid Celtic knots of shimmering abalone to the smoothness of the dark walnut wood, she loved everything about it. It was one of only two things she had ever felt to be absolutely and completely hers.

Tiffany listened for the harmony line in the Cat Stevens ballad. She slid in on the beat and kept her head down.

As it always did, the music soothed and lifted. She'd come to enjoy the rare community events when they played in the group. She knew her harp added a warmth to the sound. They occasionally tried to have her take a solo. An offer she always refused except for a few Harry Chapin songs, where she took the soulful cello part, or anything by Sting; she preferred being an accent rather than a statement.

Usually she watched the townspeople. There was always something amusing to learn, something to watch. Some were the great forces that shaped the town: Judge Slater, Gina Lamont, and Maggie Winslow—the town's second-grade teacher and a primal force for decades. Then there was the upcoming generation of Jessica, Natalya, and Becky, the self-declared overseers of the town's future. But there were other, subtler forces at play and she enjoyed watching those as well.

Tiffany had moved to Eagle Cove shortly after Ma Slater's death. Tiffany had seen right away that Peggy Naron was going to be the Judge's next wife…even though it had taken him three years to learn the same. Cal Mason Jr. and Sr., who had just married Natalya and Gina Lamont today, weren't chaotic influences. Rather, the two big men were solid, stabilizing influences to their dynamic women.

But today she didn't watch even though she could hear their laughter, pick out their voices. She kept her head down and focused on the music.

Until the moment a second guitar joined in on a chorus of the Beatles' "Here Comes the Sun." A glance to her left had her fingers jangling on the harp strings.

"Hi," Devin Robison sat cross-legged on the ground close beside her with a beautiful Martin twelve-string acoustic in his lap. He easily picked the backup line, filling in spaces between Peggy's lead and her own harmony.

"Hi," she tried in response but it came out strange and discordantly squeaky. Her fingers found their way back into the music. Once she was solid, he ducked over to the harmony himself, teasing her with a descant to her line, counterpointing the harmony. She responded by leaving him in the harmony and sliding in above Peggy's melody.

He chased her through a tricky round of rock and roll, Maroon 5 and Five for Fighting, which were always a challenge on the harp. She teased him with half harmonies in Jimmy Buffet and Fleetwood Mac, forcing him to fill in around her gaps so that the harmony line wouldn't shatter.

Only when Peggy finally called a break was Tiffany aware of how sore her fingertips were—they must have played at least a double set for them to be so sensitive. They'd played long enough for the sun to slide well down toward the ocean, making it painfully bright to look westward. Somewhere in that shining blur, the crowd began applauding wildly. All of the musicians were bowing. Even Devin had risen to his feet to join the others. Tiffany used the harp in her lap as an excuse to stay seated and simply bowed her head.

The applause went on far longer than normal. When each of the band members made a point of stopping by to shake Devin's hand and tell both him and Tiffany how wonderful their playing had been, Tiffany knew she'd messed up again. She'd always been careful to play simple harmonies, avoiding notice; but with Devin challenging her, she'd played far beyond what she normally let others see. Had her life been different, she might well have accepted the San Francisco Symphony's request for her to audition for them—one of her only regrets about abandoning her past.

As the band dispersed into the crowd, some calling for drinks, others simply heading for them, Devin remained by her side.

"I'm fine," she assured him.

"You are fine. You play wonderfully."

"I meant you can go join the others."

He shrugged as he sat back down on the grass close beside her and she couldn't help but look over at him.

"You have a nice smile." She bit down on her tongue. Tiffany had meant to compliment his playing.

"Thanks. I'm waiting for you to smile to see if you do."

"Really, I'm okay by myself." Was he flirting with her? The whole flirting thing had somehow passed her by without her ever learning how to do it.

"I don't know anyone else here."

"Oh, I'm sorry."

"Why are you sorry? You're the one person I *do* know. Other than Natalya Lamont."

He said it in a way that was funny.

"Oh," he said softly, "you don't have a nice smile."

Tiffany slapped a hand over her mouth to hide it.
"You have a *great* smile. Do it again."

# # #

Tiffany just shook her head, but her smile really was incredible. Even over the hand presently covering her mouth, Devin could see her eyes sparkling.

It made him feel as if he'd done something right. As if leaving everything he knew back in Chicago and driving into the coastal wilderness might, just might, not have been the most idiotic maneuver of his entire lifetime. Well, no, the absolutely most idiotic moment had been six weeks earlier and that had launched him on the path to Eagle Cove.

But maybe there was finally a glimmer of light in his personal tunnel.

"I'm sorry I left you with Natalya. She's mostly wonderful," Tiffany spoke from behind her covering hand.

"Except when she's teasing you?"

Tiffany nodded uncertainly, then shook her head, covering half of her face with her hair.

There were television ad shampoo models who didn't have such incredible hair. It was hard to look away from its shimmering length as it reflected Tiffany's every move and mood.

"No, Becky was teasing me. Natalya was..." Tiffany tapered off, looking puzzled.

"Protecting you," that much had been obvious.

"Really?" Her eyes went wide and her hand dropped to clutch the harp that she held against her chest like a warrior's shield. Because he was seated below her, he could see every expression despite the wide-brimmed hat... No, more than that, he could see every emotion. There was a purity that couldn't be real. Humans were never that honest. Not brothers, not ex-fiancées, and not conniving—

He shook his head, trying to shed the sudden, dark thoughts.

"She was guarding you like a mama bear," he said and liked the image though he wondered how the woman in question would feel about the description. "Natalya threatened to feed me to an orca whale."

"I have an orca-colored cat. Does that count?"

Devin laughed. "Absolutely." He almost asked if he could come see that, but decided against it at the last moment. He remembered the way she'd bolted from the upstairs bedroom— her hand had actually been shaking as she pushed the key into his palm. Shy. She was remarkably shy and it again made him wonder that she'd taken his hand in the first place. A momentary lapse? He liked being her momentary lapse.

That smile slipped back. This time he didn't comment on it for fear of scaring it away again. There was no calculation behind the smile, just a brightness to her eyes and a curve to her very nice lips. Again that strange dichotomy as she switched back and forth between seeming just a little simple and then having a quick humor. And the way she'd played, it had taken his breath away. She was beyond performance-level skilled; she should be playing concerts on international stages or something. He tried to remember if his brother's weekend band had ever been that much fun to play with before it all went so wrong, but not that he could recall.

"Excuse me?" Tiffany's voice was so soft that he'd almost mistaken it for a trick of the breeze.

"Yeah?"

"If you don't mind my asking, why are you h—" But Tiffany was cut off by a stern voice.

"Now we'll get to the bottom of this."

Devin looked up and wondered what new disaster was headed his way. The very pregnant blonde from the porch was approaching, arm in arm with a gray-haired battle-ax of a woman.

Tiffany jolted to her feet. But rather than running off, she handed her harp to him and rushed to assist the pregnant woman.

"I'm not an invalid," she protested as Tiffany and the older woman practically forced her into the seat Tiffany had just vacated. "I've got another month of this? Why didn't anyone warn me!"

Devin noted that Natalya wasn't the only over-protective one in this group as Tiffany quickly fetched the padded stool from Becky's drum kit and offered it to the gray-haired woman.

"You will not find me perching on that, Tiffany Mills."

"We'll trade," the blonde began to lever herself up.

"Sorry, Mrs. Winslow," Tiffany whispered as the older woman pushed the blonde back into her seat. "I'll get a chair from the house and—"

"I may be gray on top but I am not dead. I stand all day in the classroom," she folded her arms and glared at all three of them. "I can certainly stand here. Now sit yourself down."

In response, Tiffany sat straight down where she was standing, close beside the stool, but not on it. She ended up on the grass almost close enough for Devin to rub shoulders with her.

He silently offered her harp. She took the instrument and wrapped it protectively in her arms once more. It was as big as her torso, ornately carved, and well-used. The sweeping arch climbed past her shoulder, reaching higher than her head. He wasn't a harp aficionado, but while his Martin was one of the best commercial twelve-string guitars made, it was clear that her harp was a custom piece of a whole other class.

"Now what is this I hear?"

Devin cringed, having no idea what was about to happen.

"Jessica…"

That must be the pregnant blonde.

"…tells me that you have knowledge of what divided our town a hundred years ago."

So this wasn't about him. Still, his nerves were having trouble relaxing. Mrs. Winslow reminded him of too many dictatorial teachers from his past. Though now that her obvious displeasure was aimed elsewhere, he discovered in himself a desire to protect Tiffany just as Natalya had. Though there was something about her, that enigmatic quality to her reactions and the way she'd leapt to Jessica's aid, that made him suspect that perhaps Tiffany didn't need as much protecting as all of her friends thought. And her playing had nothing to do with timidity in any form.

Tiffany nodded reluctantly—he was learning to read her. Like her music, there were complex interactions that were as much body language as facial expression.

"A little bit longer than that actually." Then she rested her chin on the smooth curve of the neck that formed the top of the harp as if to clamp it shut.

"You know that I value our town's history."

Tiffany nodded carefully.

"And yet you did not tell me, though we've known each other two years."

"Two years, eleven months." Then Tiffany actually bit down on her lower lip and stayed very still.

"Is your reason good?" That had Jessica looking up sharply at Mrs. Winslow. She'd clearly never thought there might be a reason.

Tiffany tipped her head, rolling it enough to lean her cheek against the upsweep of the pegboard…then shrugged uncertainly.

"You will not make it too much longer," Mrs. Winslow did not make it a question.

Tiffany shook her head, but Devin could see the deep reluctance there.

The older woman considered them all for a long moment, nodded once, and turned to go.

"No, wait," Jessica called after her. "There can't be any reason for her to not tell us now what—"

"Hector Jackson," Mrs. Winslow said as she walked off, "has asked for my hand in the next dance when the band starts once more. I must find him and confirm if that is still his intent." And she was gone.

Devin couldn't help laughing. "Why in the world does she talk that way?"

"Second-grade teacher," Tiffany said quietly. So quietly that Jessica didn't hear though she sat only a few feet away.

"She was my second-grade teacher," Jessica answered in kind. "Started long before me and still is, though she's past retirement age. She wants to exemplify the English language to her students. She firmly believes that contractions will not communicate the importance of learning the language properly to young minds," Jessica sounded a little like the woman herself. "But after so many years, she can't switch it off when she's out of the classroom either."

Devin could hear the love that poured out of Jessica as she spoke. He was used to home, where people always seemed to have a hidden knife waiting in every conversation. Here people protected one another like, well, he was going to say kin, but experience had taught him that was the least true of all.

"Why would someone choose to teach second grade their whole life?"

Jessica spun on him, suddenly looking as dangerous as Natalya.

Devin held up his hands, "I meant that with nothing but respect. I just remember me in second grade and I was no blessing."

"I'll bet," her tone was as dry as the prairie in August. "Who are you?"

"Devin," he was getting tired of that question. As if everyone already knew everyone. Then he glanced at the number of wedding guests spread across the lawn and guessed that some fair portion of the town's population was here…and knew each other. And if they'd all shared the same second-grade teacher—he couldn't even guess how many second-grade classrooms there'd been at Alexander Graham Bell Elementary. That had him laughing again.

"What?" Jessica sounded only a little friendlier than the dangerous bride had been.

"I just realized that my elementary school back in Chicago was a couple times bigger than this entire town. And my high school was ten times that."

"Chicago?" Jessica lit up like he'd just said the magic password. "What part of the city?"

"North, mostly. And central," and it felt like dust on his tongue to even say that much.

"The Gaztro-Wagon," Jessica said with a happy sigh.

"The Southern Mac & Cheese Truck." Devin did miss the food already even though he'd been gone for only three days. To find another fan of the Chicago food trucks out in the wilderness of the Oregon Coast was something of a relief. Maybe civilization wasn't so far away.

"The Mexican-wrestling-mask and sombrero guys," Jessica offered next. "Their truck had a weird name."

"Tamalli Space Charros! Those guys are the best." Devin felt a sudden homesickness so deep he almost felt ill.

"No," Jessica said as if commanding him not to go there. "The Flirty Cupcakes food truck. They're the best."

And he did feel a little better for meeting her.

# # #

Tiffany had watched their reactions.

Jessica's acceptance of Devin grew rapidly based on no more than shared gastronomical experiences in a city thousands of miles away. Such simple things to tie people together. Why did she never find that? Her connections were never simple.

Devin, too, was much more complex than he'd first appeared. He shifted between joy at discovering a fellow urbanite and…Tiffany almost wondered if he was going to be sick at other moments. There was some history there that wasn't sitting comfortably. He—

"Where are you from?"

"Nob Hill, San Francisco," Devin's question surprised the answer out of her.

"Well, that explains the long hair," Jessica declared, as if San Francisco was still rooted in the 1960s and '70s.

It wasn't true. When she'd been growing up there, she'd had the same stylish haircuts as the other girls. Eventually she'd learned to dislike the attention they drew, at school and from her stepfather. She'd burned her hip clothes and grown her hair long to hide behind, but it had been too little, too late. Even after she'd managed to have him jailed, which created a major scandal for the global bank he was on the board of, she'd kept the frumpy look. By graduation she'd had the longest hair of her entire school except for two girls from India.

Last night she'd been reading her ancestor's journal that had become her guide on being a woman and come across a passage she had long since forgotten about. It directly contradicted the town legend that the town's streets had been so curiously named because the mother and daughter had fought and were no longer on speaking terms. That was the part that she had referred to when speaking with Jessica. Tiffany liked to remember Lillian's sense of humor when she was feeling sad herself.

August, 1887

Clarence loved to brush my hair. My husband was not an expressive man, but my long hair was an endless wonder to him. Now he has gone and left me with a seven-year-old daughter and a town that is little more than a dozen shacks and a bounty of timber and fish.

We are lost here in the Oregon wilderness.

But it is not in my blood to give up, not when my little Pearl grieves so. To cheer her, I have made a game. Together we have designed how the town of Eagle Cove shall someday appear. No longer a rough logging and fishing camp huddled by the bay.

We have drawn a map. Pearl has run a ruler line down the middle of the main street. "I'll name all of the streets on this side."

"Then," I told her, "I shall name all on the other."

"My half is seabirds," Pearl declared. When I indicated that she had selected the landward side of the town and yet would name it for seabirds, she did not care. "Don't use any of my names," she has commanded. Taking her instructions to heart, I have named my "half" for land birds.

Eagle Cove is only forest and clearing, so it matters not that her streets wander and curve strangely. In response, I have drawn one that follows the entire shore to the far distant bluff of Orca Head though I cannot imagine the town every reaching so far. I have named my wandering street LBB Lane, complaining that there are too many Little Brown Birds to sort out. That made my daughter's laugh ring once more in our lonely home and we are both happier for it.

The game has served its purpose and distracted her from her grief. A task well done though it fails to distract me from my own worry and grief.

I so miss the man who loved to brush my hair.

Tiffany's own hair was now as long as her ancestor's. Though there had never been a man to brush it for her. But when she brushed her own hair each night, she would pretend it was Lillian's Clarence caring for her. Of course he'd be far too old for her, well over a hundred and fifty if he'd lived, which would have made Tiffany laugh had she been alone. Her cat would appreciate the story; she made a mental note to tell Fitz tonight when she retur—

"How many in *your* high school?" Devin asked.

"Too many!" His question acted as a whiplash out of the past. There had been too many who wanted to take down the rich girl with the long hair. Too many with grasping hands who knew how to corner a shy girl and—

"Man do I know that feeling!" Devin agreed.

For a second she jolted. Had he too been—

"Feels like you're lost in a crowd."

No, he was happy.

Joking.

Which was as elusive for her as flirting.

She did her best to nod as if she'd felt the same about her school days.

After high school she'd changed her name, packed her harp and her several times great-grandmother's diary (her second cherished possession), and taken her trust-fund inheritance with her to Lewis & Clark Law School in the woods of Oregon.

She didn't go back for her stepfather's funeral after he was killed by a couple of lifers inside the jail. He'd probably bragged to the wrong person about his "conquests." Or maybe they just didn't like bankers.

Tiffany didn't go back to her mother's third high-society wedding, either.

And, though she'd considered it seriously, she also didn't go back and confront the harassers and abusers from her high school in a court of law. Though it had been very tempting, she knew that without hard evidence there was little she could do. However, she *had* listed them prominently on multiple molester sites. Several reputations had been destroyed but she refused to feel guilty, especially after other women had begun adding their own accounts to those listings.

In all of California, the only person who knew her present name and whereabouts was a lawyer who utterly despised the family lawyer. Tiffany could trust him to keep her confidence out of mere spite, completely aside from professional attorney-client privilege considerations.

"Won't get lost in the crowd here," Jessica was telling Devin. She had not departed along with Mrs. Winslow but had remained to chat, yet another skill Tiffany could wish for but had never acquired. "My graduating class had thirty-three of us."

"There he is!" Gina Lamont shouted out as she rushed up. "Devin, you made it!"

"Told you," Jessica made it an aside. "No hiding here."

Tiffany had done a fair job of that so far, but she could feel it crumbling around the edges, chipped away by good intentions of kind people. She had roots here now, roots grown from seeds planted by the discovery of the old journal in the family library. But today's revelations were more than—

"Oh good, Jessica," Gina patted her on the shoulder. "You're sitting down. Tiffany, keep an eye on her. Don't let her help with anything."

Tiffany nodded. She wouldn't have anyway.

Jessica groaned in disgust at being pampered, though she made no move to rise either.

Gina turned to inspect Devin, who was struggling to his feet. She did that to people. Her five-ten height was the only trait Gina shared with her daughter. Natalya was a dusky-skinned, slender, and dark brunette with nearly black eyes and a sharp sense of humor. Her mother was a voluptuous, blue-eyed redhead with almost as much joyous energy as Becky. She too had changed into wedding black, but with a sexy, flirty cut that must be making her new husband crazy.

Sure enough, Tiffany spotted Cal Mason Sr. crossing in their direction with his son and his new daughter-in-law in tow.

Unlike the Lamont women, the two Mason men were cut from nearly identical cloth—or perhaps baked from the same dough as they co-owned the town's bakery. (Tiffany kept her smile at the apt analogy to herself. Devin noticed far too much, as if from him she had no secrets at all.) They were both well over six feet tall and built like Swedish linebackers. In their matching charcoal-gray tuxedos, they were completely astonishing to look at. They'd have dominated any setting…that didn't have Gina and Natalya in it.

A small husky puppy trotted along behind Cal Jr. It had a good bite on its own leash.

Natalya noticed the direction of her attention, "I gave her to Cal as a wedding present."

"Damn thing is gonna chew through everything in the place," Cal Jr. said with obvious affection as he tugged back and forth on the leash to play with the dog.

Then the puppy noticed the strap on Tiffany's harp case and lunged for it. Cal scooped him up just a moment before she could cry out.

"Scamp! Should name you Gnat Jr. for your troublemaker mom." Tiffany had heard him call Natalya "Gnat"—a nickname that apparently went back to kindergarten.

"You do and you're spending your wedding night on the couch. Alone," Natalya wasn't doing a very good job of hiding her smile while making the threat.

Cal looked at the dog. "Sorry, buddy. Guess you won't get your name until tomorrow. Got me some things to do tonight."

"Such as locking up all of our shoes," Natalya tickled the puppy's nose.

"This the boy?" Cal Sr. ignored his son's and new daughter-in-law's antics as he slipped his hand around Gina's waist and looked Devin up and down. Both women looked ridiculously pleased at the attentiveness of their new husbands.

Would Tiffany look that way on her own wedding day? If she ever found someone she was willing to have a wedding with.

It was an event she'd never been able to picture clearly. Lillian Lamont's journal offered little guidance as it was not even the highlight of the day's entry:

March 1, 1879

> *Wed to Clarence Lamont by the ship's captain before he delivered us and our supplies to this unnamed strip of desolate beach close beside the Eagle River in Oregon. Though the beach is straight, I have called it Eagle Cove because I need some sense of boundary in this terrifying wilderness.*

"He is 'the boy,'" Gina confirmed, then asked, "Aren't you?"

"I think so," Devin replied calmly despite the arrival of so many new people. It was an equanimity she had never managed herself. "Of course, that depends on who you think I am."

Tiffany had been puzzling at that since his arrival. Had almost managed to ask the question herself before Mrs. Winslow's interruption. Not a guest. Hired by Gina. But he'd been given the second best room in the B&B (Gina lived in the best rooms—her ancestor's master suite). For what? She already had her summer help at the B&B lined up.

"What have you built, boy?" Cal Sr. asked.

"Now, Cal," Gina tried to stop him. "We both asked Devin plenty of questions when we interviewed and hired him."

"That was over the phone," Cal grumped. "I like to judge a man in person."

Tiffany glanced around. Natalya, Cal Jr., and Jessica were all as lost as she was. So it wasn't something that she'd missed by only coming to town twice a week for knitting group and to sell her produce.

"It's okay, ma'am," Devin told Gina, who smiled at being called "ma'am."

Devin waved a hand at the B&B.

"I've never built anything as pretty as that, but I've restored several of them. As to modern houses, I've designed a couple dozen and built them myself, or my crew did—some designs many times. Degree in architecture, but make my living as carpenter and general contractor. Wanted to build my own company to see what it was all about before joining my father's big business."

Tiffany could see the flinch. That last statement had thrown Devin at least as badly as her own admission about knowing a key piece of the town's history. But unlike her own instinct to duck and dodge, Devin continued easily and no one besides herself seemed to notice.

"Doesn't look like this old girl needs much help," he waved again to the grand Victorian, directing everyone's attention there.

But not looking himself.

Tiffany could see him watching the others cautiously, then slowly relaxing. She was glad that he didn't check in her direction.

"Oh," Cal Jr. winced at some memory as he spoke, "she has her issues now and then."

"Wimp!" His wife informed him.

"You weren't the one who had to go swimming in the basement last winter to fix the sump pump. That water was so cold that—"

"Whiner!" Natalya and her mother said in unison, then shared a smile while Cal Jr. sputtered, then Gina patted his cheek in obvious appreciation.

"Maybe I should just talk with the pup," Cal addressed the dog currently shedding fur on his dark tuxedo. "You women are dangerous." Then Cal Jr. looked down at Tiffany. "Tiffany, are you dangerous, too?"

Tiffany could feel her jaw flapping. She hadn't even realized that Cal knew her name.

"Of course she is," Jessica announced, resting a hand on Tiffany's shoulder. "Don't mess with her or you'll regret it."

Tiffany noted Jessica's smile and felt the warm squeeze on her shoulder. Tiffany wasn't dangerous, but she did like the way the tingling sensation of being included felt. Natalya, on the other hand, was the most dangerous of them all and was gearing up to renew her attack on poor Devin.

"What is he here to build then?" Tiffany tried to turn the conversation back to the safer topic. It earned her surprised looks from Natalya and Jessica that she did her best to ignore.

"You can show him on your way home," Cal Sr. dug a key ring out of his tuxedo pocket with one key on it and tossed it to Tiffany. There was a small, stamped-metal label threaded onto the same ring. *USCG Keeper's Cottage—Orca Head.* She showed it to Jessica before passing the key across to Devin.

"We purchased it from the US Coast Guard," Gina announced happily.

"Gonna be a nice annex for my wife's B&B. So you make it pretty, Devin. Deal?"

"Deal," Devin shook hands with Cal Sr. It looked very strong and manly. "But where is it?"

Tiffany pointed up at the lighthouse perched atop the rocky headland of Orca Head. "If you thought *this* house was remote…" And that's when she understood that for the first time, there would be people, well, one person, much closer to her farm than the Lamont B&B.

She was definitely going to declare her own country. And she'd install a large moat and train her cat in border patrol.

Chapter 2

*S**hould I have brought** my truck?"* Devin couldn't help looking back down the narrow lane as the B&B disappeared from sight, swallowed by the towering pine trees. He felt as if he was never going to see it again.

"Is it a four-wheel drive?"

"Sure. A Toyota pickup." They were walking in side-by-side ruts, up something Tiffany insisted on calling a road despite the deep grass and low brush that was growing between them. The woods were a profusion of thick trees, a half dozen kinds of conifers and a couple more leafy types—the only ones he recognized were maples and some variety of oak. The under- growth was so thick he wondered if a machete would even be sufficient, though farther in, deep under the pines, the way looked passable, but not along this road/path/track into the wilderness. Even the pine trees looked different than the ones in the parks back home. He really should have traveled more, but he'd never felt a need to leave the city…until it ejected him forcibly.

"Yours is the little blue SR5?"

"Uh-huh," she didn't miss anything. He'd parked among the fifty other vehicles on the far side of a line of trees, yet Tiffany had picked it out through the branches as not belonging.

"You may want to fix the road first, before trying it with that. Peggy has a road grader you can borrow."

"Peggy?"

"Small woman with red hair, married to Judge Slater." He couldn't place her, though the Judge had been hard to miss: as big as Cal Mason Sr., though not quite as tall as Cal Jr.

"And she has a road grader?"

Tiffany looked at him as if he was being stupid. Well, maybe he was. They were hiking into a wilderness that could be filled with wolves or cougars or whatever. All they were armed with was Tiffany's harp in a padded backpack case. He didn't think the Swiss army knife in his pocket would count for much in a life-and-death situation. "Music soothes the savage beast," was a misquote he'd rather not test personally.

And he was being told he could "borrow" a road grader from the Judge's wife? Had he landed in the land of the Amazons?

"I've never driven anything bigger than a Bobcat."

"Oh, I have one of those if you ever need it. Though I'm not sure I could get it from my farm to the lighthouse. I'd have to take some measurements along the trail."

"Your farm. You have a farm?"

She waved vaguely up the hill.

"Up here?" Now Devin himself could hear how stupid he was sounding. He wasn't used to being so out of his depth. Today was being a harsh lesson.

"Farther back," Tiffany didn't explain more. "But this is where you'll be working."

The path crested the ridge and at first he didn't see what she was talking about as the trees to the east were still thick as could be.

But to the west, toward the ocean, there was a broad clearing along the top of the ridge. There were small saplings, the size to be planted in a Chicago suburban front yard to make it look finished. Here they were tiny things that looked as if they needed to be either mowed down or pulled up like weeds from among the tall grass.

At the far end of the clearing, a towering lighthouse utterly commanded the point. It was a classic: circular, white, and several stories tall with a glass housing at the top. Inside, he could see a big glasswork lens spinning. Each time it swung by, there was a bright flash of the light.

"Why is it flashing? It's still daylight."

"It's a navigation beacon, so it's always flashing. At night I like to watch it as it sweeps across the trees then out over the water. When there is a light sea mist, it's an amazing sight, like the beams of light could go on forever." Tiffany's eyes had gone soft and wondering. Again, that simple child inside what he was coming to understand was not a simple woman. She noticed his scrutiny and continued flatly. "White, green, and red every ten seconds. They're all automated now so the keepers don't live by the lights anymore."

Sure enough. He watched the lighthouse through a full minute, two flashes of each color. It *was* mesmerizing. The light itself didn't move or blink as he'd always assumed. Instead, a stepped lens bigger than his torso spun about it, six of them actually, forcing the light into beams. It was the glass itself that was colored.

Then he refocused in the foreground. To the north side of the clearing, providing it with a nice southern exposure, stood the lighthouse keeper's cottage. It was right out of some storybook: two stories tall, a big box with six well-spaced windows wide, all painted in glaring white with a red shingle roof. If ever there was a blank template, this was definitely it. He would need to keep the feel or it would lose its lighthouse charm. But he needed to do something serious, because other than its lighthouse heritage, it was one of the least charming buildings he'd ever seen.

"What do you know about—" Devin turned, but he was alone. There was no sign that only moments ago Tiffany had stood here beside him. He saw no hint in the trees, no flash of color from her dark blue harp carrying case. He scanned again, but he was definitely alone. He couldn't even see any sign of a trail leading away other than the one back to the B&B. A vague hint of what must once have been a logging road switchbacked to the north. Yet she'd waved southeast toward her farm and in that direction there was nothing but a solid wall of forest and dense undergrowth.

Still no sign. He pulled the key out of his pocket and headed over for a closer inspection of the cottage.

Devin just hoped to hell that he hadn't imagined her. He was less concerned for his mental state of possibly hallucinating and much more concerned with hoping she was real so that he could meet her again.

# # #

Tiffany stood fifty feet into the trees to the east of the lighthouse clearing and watched Devin Robison.

She knew that her abrupt departure was rude, but she hadn't been able to stop herself. She had spoken more and to more people today than she typically did in a month. But what had finally driven her to escape was how much she'd enjoyed speaking with Devin. Despite his obvious pain over something in his recent past, there was an easiness to being around him. She'd always suspected that her own pain pushed others away and isolated her. Perhaps it was sharing a common theme of broken pasts which had made him so easy to be with.

It was the very easiness that she found so disconcerting.

Tiffany almost called out to him as he kept turning again and again to look for her. It was touching really. When at long last he went into the keeper's cottage, she picked up the compound bow and quiver of arrows—that she carried for protection but never took into town—from where she kept them stashed before turning for home. She brought it with her ever since a black bear had almost caught her. She'd escaped only by shedding her pack of fresh supplies and bolting for the farm. Coming back with the bow had filled her larder with bear meat to make up for the loss of her slashed and chewed supplies, but her pack had never been the same no matter how she patched it.

Keeping to the narrow path she'd forged, little wider than a deer trail and mostly over rock outcroppings, she left little trace of her passage. That had been her goal, her guiding principle since her arrival in Oregon, long before she came to Eagle Cove. She wanted no one to know where she had passed, or how.

At first she had appreciated the privacy. She had attended no functions in town. Spoke with no one and slowly learned to enjoy the peace. Even now, the birdsong soothed her far more than any people. Gray squirrels, little Douglas browns with the tufted ears, and striped chipmunks scattered up trees, saw it was her, and came back down hoping for a treat.

"No treats today, girls. Tuesday, I promise." When she went to town, she normally slipped an extra scone or a few cookies into her pocket, especially the ones with nuts and raisins, but she'd forgotten them in all of the day's flurry. A few of the braver ones followed her the distance of two or three trees before moving away to more fruitful pastures.

Going to town. She'd thought of it as if doing so was a normal thing. When had that happened?

Three years ago her ancestor's journal had led her to Eagle Cove and it had taken Tiffany months to work up the nerve to enter the town. She hadn't wanted to even then, but her assistant had finished his job and left. Everyone had assumed he was her boyfriend and that he'd jilted her and stolen her truck, leaving her abandoned and penniless. Actually, she'd bought him the truck as part of his pay. In exchange, he'd spent three months helping her with the heavy work of getting the farm started—a back-breaking summer before he'd returned to college.

She felt bad about leaving the false assumptions from the rumor in place. But Tiffany had learned the hard way, the true danger of anyone knowing she was descended from the highest tier of the San Francisco financial monarchy. Any misdirection was welcome.

Her four-times-great-grandmother had made a fortune in big lumber in the late 1800s. The guardian of her three-times-great-grandmother had owned the first lumber ship to arrive after the 1906 quake and fire and had quickly chartered two more. Three more generations of women had safeguarded that fortune assiduously. But for her mother's ability to marry well, much of it would have slipped away in the last generation prior to Tiffany's own. But she did marry well, and it had continued to grow. And Tiffany had wanted no part of it.

Her entrance into Eagle Cove society had been tentative. By the first time she came down from the woods to buy some essentials at the Warbler Market, she'd had "eccentric" down (though she wished it felt more like an act than a reality) and had been reluctant to break it.

One day she'd been slipping along the verge of the Lamont B&B's property, she'd stopped to look at it. This was the house that Lillian Lamont had built for her first daughter, Pearl, so that she would be close beside her mother. Lillian had lived in the house next door, now owned by Judge Slater. There was so much history and so many memories here. It was like a lens into the past.

January 1, 1900

New Year's Day

We held the housewarming at Pearl's upon the first day of the new century. Together we have designed and had built a Victorian house close beside our family home so that we may never live far apart.

Each visitor brought a log and we toured through the new house until each fireplace had been filled and lit. The warmth of the air felt almost as great as the warmth of spirit shared by those within these new walls.

My daughter is situated now, though her hopes for Thomas Harrow to join her were so recently cut short by the loss of his fishing craft. Yet we Lamont women put on our cheerful faces and welcomed all who came to wish her well. She is only nineteen, but in the morning she sails to San Francisco. There she shall briefly reside with my aging mother. I have entrusted Pearl with renewing our lucrative timber and fish sale contracts.

It is my hope that she will find a better man than poor Thomas while she is about her duties.

And Tiffany had seen the two layers, both past and present, intertwine that day three years ago as she walked by the B&B. She had been pulled toward the grand Victorian, fascinated by the vision of men and women once so attractively dressed in their Sunday finery, visiting good wishes upon the town's founders. She edged forward, imagining that she could catch a glimpse of Lillian and Pearl Lamont at their very best.

Then Tiffany had stumbled against the first step up to the verandah. The image faded, she was once again in the present, and she stood mere feet from a circle of women knitters, sitting out on the porch in the spring sunshine. The bright clicking of aluminum needles manipulating colorful and patterned yarns was so startling that she couldn't move.

Her hesitation lasted too long and Mrs. Winslow had spotted her. She'd waved Tiffany to sit in a seat beside her in such a peremptory fashion that Tiffany had been unable to refuse. But once there, they had allowed her to simply sit with her hands clenched around a glass of ice tea. The others might have looked at her oddly; she didn't know because she hadn't looked up. They let her just listen, and hear the warm friendship that flowed back and forth between them all.

Weeks later, working up her nerve, she'd come to town on a Tuesday afternoon with her own knitting tucked in her pack. Daring greatly, she'd walked up onto the porch, sat down next to Maggie Winslow, and pulled out her own project. The conversation had died at first, but once it restarted, Maggie Winslow had leaned over and whispered in her gruff way, "Good girl." That had made her Tiffany's first friend in town…her first in *years*. Though it was weeks before she could find her voice to answer back, she'd never forget that day or that kindness.

Tiffany stopped high on the trail leading to her farm and looked back to the north. The trail crested here on a ridge. It was one of the best views there was of the town founded by her forebears. Two miles to the north lay Eagle Bay, where the Eagle River pooled and slowed before finally reaching the sea. Beyond it lay only state forestland, patchworked with recent loggings and more mature growths.

The town stretched for two miles southward along the beach from the docks. The core of town lay nestled close by Eagle Bay. Residential areas stretched a half mile inland then were backed by a few small farms and the gravel-runway airport. The houses continued close above the beach to the south, finally petering out in the last long stretch of LBB Lane, slipping between the ocean and the forest to reach the Lamont B&B.

Her perch was at twice the height of Orca Head here and she could look down on the lighthouse and the cottage. Devin stepped out of the door as she watched and she could imagine him looking for her one more time as he twisted and turned— though he didn't look high enough to see her perch above the ridge—before he hurried down the trail, racing back down toward the civilization of the B&B. Evening was fast approaching and clearly the forest unnerved him. Yet another reason to feel bad about abandoning him.

"Sorry, Devin." It was the first time she'd said his name aloud and she liked the sound of it. Then she felt utterly ridiculous. She'd met many men with wonderful voices and learned that it didn't mean a thing about who they were. Devin's voice was nice—not deep, but nice. Kind with a bit of funny built in.

He disappeared out of sight down the trail after one last look behind.

"Devin."

Perhaps it was ridiculously schoolgirl, but she still liked the sound of his name.

She turned south, crossing over the ridge and out of sight of Eagle Cove. More importantly, out of sight of the lighthouse as well. Tiffany began to trot along the trail despite how it made the harp thump against her back. The farm might not be her own country…yet, but it felt as if it was. Her step always lightened as it came into view.

"Returning to her remote kingdom," she announced to the forest. After all, no one said her new country had to be a democracy.

"By unanimous accolade," she told a pair of seagulls riding high on the updrafts, "she is acclaimed the ruler. Long live Queen Tiffany Mills."

Giggling to herself, she went to feed the cat. Fitz always pouted if she wasn't greeted immediately upon Tiffany's return… or much more importantly, fed precisely on time.

# # #

Devin tried to relax, but he felt twitchy and couldn't seem to pull it off. He kept turning to look over his shoulder as if Tiffany would suddenly reappear out of thin air, just as she'd disappeared into it. It wasn't doing him any good because he sat on the small bench on the B&B's verandah where he'd first met her. And that meant that the only thing over his shoulder was the outside wall of the Lamont B&B. In front of him, the evening had swallowed the front lawn and chased the last of the wedding guests inside.

Light came from the windows behind him and the multi-colored twinkle lights wrapped about an old cherry tree that commanded the center of the yard. Lurking in the shadows, great trunks of trees soared upward into the darkness. He'd have to ask what they were…he didn't think redwoods grew here, but what did he know.

Somewhere beyond that was the steady roar of the freeway.

Except there was no freeway, but there was definitely a steady roar. Not a train; the rhythm was wrong. Besides, he'd seen no tracks as he came into town. He twisted and turned before he identified the source.

The ocean! It was a long, steady thunder in the darkness. Yet another strangeness of this odd place he'd landed in. A moment later his ears again told him that they were listening to the Kennedy Expressway as if I-90 was running close by. He wondered when his ears would catch up to the Oregon Coast like the rest of him.

"You're sitting in her favorite spot, you know," Becky dropped down on the bench beside him.

"Whose?" Apparently his brain was still somewhere in Chicago along with his hearing. He could see why Tiffany liked it. It offered a wide view, but it placed his back to a wall, with another to his right because of a jog in the architecture. It was partially protected from the wind…and from people approaching an obviously shy woman from too many directions at once.

"I do so love a wedding," Becky ignored his question and bubbled on. "I never thought I would, you know. But once you have one of your own, it just makes the world seem so much brighter."

Or *darker*. But Devin had learned to keep such thoughts to himself.

"And a *double* wedding…" Becky sighed happily.

"Are you close?"

"With Natalya? We go back almost to the hospital room. All three of us;. Jessica and Natalya are cousins, which I always envied, and tall, which I *really* envied. And now we're all married. I don't think I could stand it if I was and they weren't. It's so amazing to be back together again."

"Jessica was in Chicago?" Devin had been so pleased to find someone who knew his hometown. And at the same time, it had thrown him badly to be reminded of the places and flavors. In all likelihood he'd be back there in the fall. This was just a summer job after all, but he had no idea how he'd ever face that, especially not in four short months.

"She went and stayed ten years, the dizzy girl. She was following in the footsteps of Mrs. Winslow, who was a journalist there, back when *she* was young…if you can imagine Maggie Winslow ever being young," she confided the last in a whisper and then giggled like a little girl rather than a married woman in her early thirties. "I mean she was probably only my age or a little more when I had her in second grade. And that is a totally weird thought. But to a seven year old girl, all adults are ancient."

"I'm out here shopping for a retirement home myself," Devin tried to crack his voice with age. Though it was hard to imagine anyone thinking of Becky as ancient. She bubbled with enthusiasm, more than most kids he'd met.

"Eagle Cove is the best place there is. I never left, not like Natya and Jess."

"Why?" That came out harsher than he intended. "Aren't you curious what's out there?" He waved a hand, but not toward distant Chicago. Not that he'd traveled or explored either, but Chicago was much closer to the center of the universe than Eagle Cove.

"Sure. But I have a life here, friends, and my brewery, even before I made an honest man of Harry. I'm sure I'll travel someday. I would love to taste the German and British brews in their own locales, but this is home. Why would I look any further?"

Devin didn't have a good answer to that one, because Chicago certainly didn't feel like home anymore.

Behind him, the party continued. The cracked-open windows allowed the sound of conversation and laughter to filter out and join the ocean's roar—his ears must have finally caught up with him. He was just wondering why Becky was out here with him rather than inside with the others when a tall man with blond hair stepped out onto the porch.

"There you are."

"I've been waiting for you," Becky made a sudden show of rubbing at her arms and shivering as if she was suddenly in a chill Arctic winter rather than a warm spring evening. "I can't believe it took you almost five minutes to notice I was gone." Then she stopped shivering and winked at Devin as if he'd been party all along to her little tease.

"It took me less than a minute, but then I had to find your jacket, and after that I had to convince Jessica that I was indeed going to find you if she'd just stop delaying me. Now I want my dance with you."

Becky took the jacket and set it on the bench between her and Devin.

"See why I love the man," Becky told him, then offered another of her happy sighs as she took her husband's hand and bounced to her feet. "If you'll excuse us, we have a tradition of dancing in the dark after weddings. Call Marty if we fall off the cliff edge."

"Marty?"

"He's the town policeman," Harry answered. "I think he's in the kitchen with his wife and Jessica's parents."

And he led her far out onto the lawn past the glow from the cherry tree's twinkle lights. Then the two indistinct shadows became one and they began to dance ever so slowly. Thankfully nowhere near the high-bank cliff over the beach.

The town policeman. Singular. Devin didn't even know how many *precincts* Chicago had.

Devin could practically hear Becky's contented sigh from here on the porch.

And then he had the strangest image of him and Tiffany dancing beneath the stars. He barely knew her. Had never touched her, except—he flexed his hand at the memory—as she'd led him across the kitchen and minutes later when she'd pressed the room key into his palm as she fled. Yet somehow he could easily imagine what it would feel like to hold her against him. There would be a warmth and a genuineness that Devin had rather doubted existed until his arrival in Eagle Cove. She would feel…right.

Not like Rebecca, who no one would ever dare to call Becky. Rebecca Monica Monash of the Winnetka Monashs. When he'd held Rebecca, he'd always been aware that she wasn't to be "mussed up." Apparently there was no tragedy worse than a woman being "mussed up" in public…or in private. Five-foot-five of elegant blonde, an exquisite horsewoman, and always dressed in designer clothes—in public, in private, and even in the bedroom.

In retrospect he had no idea what he'd ever seen in Rebecca Monica Monash of Sheridan Road, except perhaps that she was the woman that everyone wanted. And his family, the Robisons, had the connections and wealth that met her requirements. Devin had been, perhaps still was though he wasn't sure anymore, the heir apparent to the Robison construction empire. That had assured him of Rebecca's juggernaut-strong attention.

Right up to the moment where he'd proven the old adage that it was bad luck to see the bride in her wedding dress. Or at least half in it.

Devin had stumbled upon her just an hour from the altar, her dress peeled down to her waist, her Prada lingerie filmy over her fair skin—one breast elegantly displayed and the other hidden by where his couldn't-keep-a-job older brother's face was buried. And when Rebecca had spotted Devin, she'd met his gaze levelly, still cradling Mikal's head as if to say, "Of course this is a part of our marriage."

Apparently all other men bent to her will.

Devin had considered bowing out and merely leaving her at the altar.

Instead, he'd pulled out his phone, snapped a picture of Rebecca Monica Monash's "mussed-ness" as her expression shifted into shock. He had posted it to his social feeds as he walked out the back door of the cathedral with the caption, "I guess the wedding is off."

The backlash had been immense. The Monashs, who should have been horrified or at least embarrassed, had defended their "little girl." His own mom, who served on several committees with Mrs. Monash insisted he should apologize, announce that it was a "Photoshop joke in bad taste," and then go through with the wedding to make everything right. His dad had shrugged, "Hell, your mother and I have never been saints. Nobody ever said you had to fuck the woman you married. My secretary has the hots for you. Go ease yourself there. Trust me, she's good at that."

Devin shuddered, trying to shake off the image.

The cool Oregon evening *did* suddenly feel cold.

Devin stumbled to his feet. Left Becky and her husband to their intimate dance in the night.

He'd come so close to revealing that he was next in line to the control of one of America's largest contractors, a fact he'd kept carefully hidden even during the job interview. He needed to be away from his family, and from their business and his own. When he'd spotted the tiny ad—"experienced renovation contractor needed, Oregon Coast"—he'd immediately pulled out his phone and dialed.

Only getting lost twice in the odd twists and turns of the Victorian, he found his way to his third floor room and pitched face first into bed.

# # #

Tiffany had been in too much of a state last night to do more than lock the chickens into the coop before going to bed. And she hadn't read a word of her four-times-great-grandmother Lillian's journal, something she typically did every night.

The wedding had slid into her veins and made her blood flow faster—or perhaps in tiny whirlpools. Natalya and Gina had looked so beautiful as they stood at the rose arbor, which the two grooms had somehow transported from Mrs. Winslow's cloistered garden for the ceremony. So much joy and hope combined together.

Eagle Cove was no paradise, the Judge dealt with divorces as often as any judge did. But when it was special, there was no mistaking it, and last night had been doubly so.

She awoke with the first light of dawn filtering down from the circular plastic dome atop her yurt. The circular space of her open floor plan was barely visible as she dressed, but the warm woods of the structure were always a joy, even in dim light. The sidewall was made of seven-foot-high latticework that looked far too frail to hold up the structure. But the dozens of polished, long rafters speared up into the central ring to support the sealed canvas roof. So different from Devin's Victorian bedroom at the B&B.

When designing the living space, she had chosen simplicity in style, function over form. A sectioned-off bath was the only enclosed area. With a line of bookcases, she'd separated off a workshop including tools, gardening supplies, and medicines she needed for the goats and chickens. Most of the space was a full kitchen, a queen-sized bed (and she still hadn't finished the new quilt she'd intended for it), and a comfortable living/dining room in front of the two big windows looking out over her meadow and the ocean. A propane stove with a glass front kept her warm and provided a cheery flame.

Fitz watched her with on sleepy eye from the other pillow on her bed for a while before going back to sleep. Morning tea in hand, she stepped out onto the wide deck and descended the redwood steps in the first light of dawn. Her farm was still in deep shadows, but to the south and west the smooth ocean rolled in endless waves to the horizon. Even as she stood and breathed in the pine and sea salt-scented air, she could see the light changing, shifting from dark blue to soft pink along the horizon.

Some mornings the sun lit the entire horizon and this was one. No offshore fogbank today as there would be in summer. No storm clouds building at the first sign of land after their long journey over the ocean—preparing to unleash their load of rain.

She'd built the chicken coop under the raised platform for her yurt—which, she'd learned the hard way, had been a huge mistake. She didn't mind the occasional night clucking of the chickens, but it had required a lot of sound insulation to keep the rooster's call from electrifying her like a Taser every morning. She'd tried any number of solutions, but a yurt's walls were thin and did nothing to muffle sound. The final solution had been to install lightproof shutters over the henhouse windows and remember to close them each night.

Sure enough, the moment she cracked the first one open, Dillinger—he of the lethal crow—let loose his morning salvo. In moments, the chickens were up and about and declaring the start of their day. She opened the door and they poked their heads out to inspect the pen she'd constructed as if they'd never seen it before.

"Brains of a pea," she chided them as they clucked about her feet while she scattered feed. The pen had chicken wire around the sides and fishnet (interlaced with orange tape) over the top.

Jake, the bachelor bald eagle, just molting from his juvenile brown-headed year into his trademark white head, soared low, looking like the raggedy teen that he was. His head feathers were half brown, half white, and always seemed to be sticking out at odd angles. Every day he carefully checked her chicken protection for gaps.

"Get along, you chicken eagle." The tease always worked—Jake soared higher into the brightening day to find easier pickings and was gone. He hunted a lot among the field by the lighthouse, though he could drag twenty inches of salmon out of the bay when he put his mind to it.

Between yesterday and today she'd gained four new chicks. She swiped two fresh-laid eggs for her morning omelette that dressed up nicely with the addition of an early wild morel mushroom she'd found yesterday morning and a sprinkle of homemade goat cheese.

Then she rushed off to check on the goat pen. It was a temporary fence that she moved around the land to wherever she wanted the undergrowth cleared. The Forest Service, not knowing about the mistake in property lines, had clear-cut eight of her ten acres five years before she bought it. This had turned out to be a huge bonus. She had a two-acre buffer of forest from the nearest passable road, and eight acres of cleared land to work.

She simply moved the pen about and the pygmy goats mowed down the tall grass, chomping the salal, blackberries, and alder shoots flush to the dirt. On quiet days she'd take them all out on a walk to some particularly lush area and read a book while they grazed.

With a clucking sound, Tiffany warned Tall Guy that she was coming. The massive Kangal lumbered to his feet. Two and a half feet tall at the withers, the brindle-furred guard dog trotted eagerly up to the fence's gate to await her. She let herself through and he leaned his big head into the center of her chest. She gave him a big scritch, which had him mumbling happily to himself. Then he raised his head to glance wistfully over her shoulder at the steel can outside the fence.

"Fibber! You said you loved me!" He raised his great, sad eyes set in his broad, black face. "Oh, like you're starving to death."

But she scooped up his dog bowl and carried it back out to the can to fill it with dog food. She really needed to write and thank the woman who'd told her about Kangals. Donna had kept the full-sized Nubian goats and a Kangal. They weren't shepherds, they were guard dogs. They could take down a coyote, even a couple of them, and would brave a bear, spooking it back into the woods. The big dogs were quite content to live with their flock, even when the flock was so much shorter than they were. A pygmy goat rarely reached two feet at the withers.

While Tall Guy ate, she circulated among the goats. Her *Little Women* were doing fine. Meg and cousin Flo were about to drop kids. Jo, Beth, Amy, and their friend Annie already had. Tiffany had decided it would be too crass to name her rutting male Laurie; she'd needed a scandalous lout. Horatio snorted at her out of both nostrils, which had earned him his Horatio Hornblower moniker. He swaggered about, firm in the belief that he was somehow in charge of his little harem. With all of the females bearing, Horatio had certainly lived up to his duties.

She started checking the goats more carefully. Trimming hooves, inspecting teeth, and so on. They were used to the routine and it gave her a chance to interact with each one. Only Horatio made any fuss, nibbling at the untucked hem of her flannel work shirt, which he knew was forbidden.

# # #

Devin had woken a dozen times in the night, wondering at the expressway's roar, only to remember he was nowhere near the Kennedy or the LSD. Lake Shore Drive was two thousand miles away. He'd finally watched the moon set into the ocean just an hour before dawn.

He hadn't expected to find Gina Lamont in the kitchen starting breakfast.

"Aren't you on your honeymoon?"

"Nope," Gina handed him a large mug of coffee. "Cal Jr. and Cal Sr. run the town bakery together, so we tossed a coin and Senior and I took our honeymoon the week before the wedding."

"Oh," Devin sipped the coffee and settled at the small booth seat so that he'd be out of her way after his offer of assistance was refused. "I guess that means that your daughter got stuck with all of the final wedding arrangements."

"Exactly!" Gina sounded very pleased as she added link sausages to a hot pan. In seconds, the aroma had his mouth watering. "Though I am keeping it simple this morning. I have some frozen strawberries, which I'm using to make waffles with a mascarpone and maple syrup topping, and a side of Apple Brown Betty."

"If that's your idea of simple, I'm never leaving."

She waved a spatula at him, "Be careful of what you ask for in this town, Devin Robison. Statements like that can lead you in strange directions." She smiled down at her sausages. Goofy morning-after-wedding looked good on her. "My Cal certainly changed my direction and now I wonder what I was doing with the years up until now. I never dreamed that I'd ever marry."

As to dreams, Devin didn't have a whole lot of those anymore, so he didn't think that would be an issue. A few months spent as far as he could get from Chicago was good enough for him.

"What I got for my dreams," Gina continued as she checked the baking Brown Bettys, "was a man who took me on a week-long dogsled tour in Fairbanks, Alaska, and thought it was a great honeymoon surprise."

Devin almost snorted his next sip of hot coffee.

"Worse, it was wonderful! I can't stand that he was right. A man isn't supposed to do something like that to a woman who has been single all her life."

"But Natalya…" was her daughter—at least that's what everyone said. He decided that a subject change was in order. "Tiffany said I could borrow a road grader from someone named Peggy?"

And that was how an hour later he found himself, with a bellyful of waffles and Apple Brown Betty, across town at the small rural airport, knocking on the door of a big hangar.

"Gina called about my grader," was the greeting that met him. "Come on," and she led the way into the shadowed hangar.

Peggy was just as Tiffany had described her: short and darkly redheaded. Which had left out everything else. She was at least sixty, had unabashed streaks of gray in her red hair, walked with a rolling gait like a cowboy or a Navy sailor, and had deep blue eyes that he was fairly sure could see right through him.

He knew nothing about small planes, but the assembled biplane just inside the hangar door looked classic and in mint condition. The unassembled one? He could barely tell that it was a plane. The broad hangar floor was scattered with a vast array of bits and pieces. He spotted some metalwork in the shape of wings, but with no coverings on them. An airframe in sections. An improbably large engine half disassembled onto pallets. But it wasn't chaos. It was like one of those exploded views, everything laid out just so. Peggy radiated competence even just walking across the hangar, so he had no doubt that she was the one rebuilding it.

There was also a small helicopter and a large RV parked in the back. The road grader was parked between the RV and the hangar wall. It too was a classic. A Cat 112F, which he'd only ever seen in the equipment junkyard catalogs. It had to be sixty years old, though the paint was fresh and there were no signs of leaking hydraulic fluid anywhere.

"She's one of the first two hundred of the four thousand they built," Peggy patted the big machine as if it were a kitten. "She doesn't have a lot of the upgrades of the later models, but she runs like a champ. I use her mostly to keep the gravel runway smooth. It'll be good for her to stretch her legs out in the hills a bit."

Devin had run small excavators and a Cat D2 dozer, which was little more than a Bobcat in serious need of a weight loss program. They were small, chunky crawlers with enough power to completely reshape a residential backyard. But this road grader was nearly thirty feet long, ten high, with a twelve foot wide scraping blade dangling between the front tires and the rest of the machine. More significantly, the D2 had very little imagination and minimal controls to match. The road grader had a proliferation of controls—the blade alone had angle, depth, tilt, reach, and who knew what else. The back wheels didn't even have to follow the front wheels because there was an articulation joint in the middle so that the main machine could run down the level road while the nose of the beast skewed up hills and over ditches.

His protests were ignored and his suggestion that she might want to do it for him was met with, "Got a flight today." But he wasn't so sure about that. Something in her smile said that he was going to be driving the machine no matter what, so he stopped arguing and tried to absorb everything she gave him in a twenty minute lesson on how to run the grader.

"Last thing," she called out as he managed to find the first of six forward gears, without accidentally finding one of the six reverse gears. "This model doesn't have rollover protection, so if you flip her, be sure to jump well clear." Her face was absolutely deadpan before she turned away. He wondered how long she was going to hold the laugh in…hopefully until he was out of earshot.

He lurched off along the runway and onto the road leading through town.

No question what stories would be told in the local bar tonight. As he drove toward town, every single person who saw him coming started to raise a hand to wave, then froze with a puzzled expression on their face.

Eagle Cove was so small that everyone knew who was supposed to be driving the road grader. He was trying not to feel too self-conscious about everyone staring at him perched atop Peggy's big machine, and that's when he made his first mistake…and then his second.

He managed to find the transmission release and the brake before he could make a third.

Devin's first mistake had been turning onto Gull Way. Not yet comfortable with reverse, he'd forged ahead. Navigating up and down the hills had taught him a great deal about where to find third and fourth gear while going down the hills, and first and second for climbing slower than he could walk.

Mistake Two: to eventually escape the hills of Gull Way, he'd turned onto Shearwater Lane, which was flat but wasn't much wider than the road grader itself. It had deep ditches down one side that he'd bet would roll the machine if he slipped into one.

"Are you lost, Mr. Robison?"

It took him a moment to find the speaker. It was the woman who had practically attacked Tiffany…Winslow. Maggie Winslow, the second-grade teacher, was standing beside her car in her driveway—which he'd just completely blocked. He shrugged uncertainly. The town only had a few dozen roads; everything this side of Beach Way was named for sea birds, most of which he'd never heard of. That made them far too easy to mix up. At least he assumed a shearwater was a bird, because everything else in all of Eagle Cove seemed to be named that way.

"Take a right at the end of the street. That is Egret Hollow. Do not turn onto Sandpiper Circuit until you learn to drive much better than you presently do." With that she climbed into her car, clearly ready for him to move along.

He just didn't know if he dared.

"I'll give you a hand," a man called out from a driveway on the other side of the road. He paused to pat two seriously cute twins on the head and plant a very thorough kiss on the knockout wife that was the spitting image of her children. Or the other way around. Devin's thoughts were getting decidedly scrambled.

"Don't let Dragon Winslow spook you," he called out as he headed down the road ahead of Devin and waved him forward.

"I heard that, Vincent McCall," she called from her open car window.

"Wouldn't have been any fun if you didn't, ma'am," Vincent said it with absolute respect.

Devin found first gear and eased away from the two driveways. With Vincent's help, he navigated the turn without landing in any ditches or running over Vincent. Unwilling to try any of the higher gears or try to fit the big machine into a single lane, Devin walked the road grader mostly down the center of the road and screwed up traffic in both directions.

# # #

"You grow the most beautiful vegetables, Tiffany."

She kept her silence as Greg sorted her produce atop one of the big steel prep tables in the back of the Puffin Bay Diner. Greg and his father the Judge always made her a bit nervous. The Judge was an austere, silent man, and she felt like a trespasser every time she entered his kitchen. Greg was an amazing chef, or so everyone said; she'd never eaten one of his dinners. And he always complimented her produce.

"Winter beets, spring leeks, fresh spinach, and snow peas. I can't believe you grow snow peas. This gives me some great ideas for tomorrow night, you really must come at least once." Greg had recently added a Tuesday night dinner at The Puffin.

His father served breakfasts at the Puffin Bay Diner five days a week. His son turned it into The Puffin on Friday and Saturday nights—fixed menu, fixed price (very high). But not wanting to shut out the locals who had helped him get started, he'd recently added a "locals only" Tuesday night. It was back to the original tradition: stuff a twenty in the jar, if you can afford it, and Greg took care of the rest.

"Seriously, Tiffany. No charge. Anytime you want."

She nodded, a little abashed by his generosity couldn't figure out how to explain that she had no need of charity, however kind.

When he didn't continue, she tipped up her head enough to see his face beyond the brim of her hat. He was waiting.

"I—" she waved a hand to the south. "My farm. Long way at night." She sounded like a babbling fool, typical of her when in town. It was as if by being silent for so long she'd forgotten how to talk to people at all.

Tiffany heard the big truck engine.

"Will you look at that?" Someone called from the front of the diner. Soon everyone was moving to stare out the front windows. Laughter was beginning to sound throughout the diner.

Not wanting to join the crowd as Greg and the Judge were, Tiffany slipped out the back door and saw the problem…or at least half of it.

The back end of Peggy's road grader was still in the street beside the diner. The front end was out on Beach Way. It sat at a dead stop. Even as she watched, it jerked forward about two feet, slammed to a stop, then stalled.

Devin leaned forward over the steering wheel as if he was going to cry.

Through the open back door into the kitchen, she could still hear the laughter and exclamations from the crowd in the dining room. She could see others gathering on the street to watch him.

Tiffany knew how that felt. The creeping truth that you could do nothing right and the sick feeling that came with it and pressed in while others watched. Her heart couldn't bear to watch his pain.

She closed the back door and slipped up to the open door of the grader's cabin.

"Devin?"

"Just shoot me now, Tiffany. Please?"

"I'll bring my bow and arrow next time."

He raised his head and looked down at her. "You have a bow and arrow?"

She wouldn't have said so if she didn't.

"Uh, I'll remember not to upset you. Do you hunt with it, too?"

"Elk and deer. Coyotes if my dog doesn't scare them off. Though I only started carrying it when I had an argument with a bear."

"You argued with a bear?" What planet created women like this? Rebecca Monica Monash of Sheridan Road never argued with anything bigger than a designer label at Fields. "Dare I ask who won?"

Tiffany simply looked at him.

"Okay, you're here. Where's the bear?"

"Salted jerky. I don't have a freezer, so I had to preserve it another way. And I sold some to Greg, a chef in town." She waved to the building behind her. A careful glance and she saw that the audience was no longer pressing up against the glass and the street was emptying once more as people went back to their meals and errands.

"Can I go back to Chicago now?"

"I don't think Peggy would like it if you don't return her grader first."

Devin rested his head back down on the steering wheel. "If that's the case, then I'm not sure I can ever leave."

# # #

Devin watched as Tiffany walked once around the grader before coming to stand once more by the cabin door. Her eyes were the soft blue-gray of a hazy summer sky. Unlike Rebecca's coolly perfect blue eyes the color of a frozen winter sky. He felt as if Tiffany was seeing him, actually looking at him rather than her own reflection in his face.

"I think…" she glanced along the vast length of the grader. "I think you should teach me how to drive that machine."

"But I don't *know* how to drive that beast. I can't even turn it."

"I saw," and her smile lit up her face more brightly than the music had yesterday.

"Great." Exactly what his ego hadn't needed.

"Teach me anyway." Then she climbed up beside him.

The bench seat wasn't all that wide. Even though she was slender, they were touching shoulder to shoulder and hip to hip. And rather than being totally distracting, he found it to be a calming, focusing feeling.

"I'm ready."

At a loss for what else to do, he started on the far left and began explaining each control and what it did. And the more he explained, only occasionally redirected by her quiet questions, the better he understood how they interacted.

For half an hour they sat there, blocking the main intersection in town. There were no honked horns. No shouts of complaint. People backed up and went around the block to get by him. He didn't know where he was, but it definitely wasn't Chicago, where he'd be ticketed, towed, and possibly shot by this point.

# # #

Gina waved as they edged by the B&B. It had taken Devin another half hour to drive the two miles from town and news traveled much faster in Eagle Cove than that.

Tiffany had considered having him shift up to third gear, but if second was all he was comfortable with, she wouldn't push him.

He set the blade at the base of the road up to the lighthouse. It barely knocked down the small bushes and it certainly never touched the soil. After fifty feet, she nudged the blade-depth lever with one finger until it bit in.

"You sure?" Devin asked tightly.

Tiffany glanced down at the blade now scraping across the grass. It clanged loudly on a rock. "I was going to suggest we go even deeper, but I'm not sure." By halfway up she was sure but wasn't willing to change anything as they reached the first switchback.

Devin negotiated it without driving them off the edge and down into a stream's deep ravine.

As they broke into the high meadow in front of the lighthouse, Jake the eagle swooped very low along the other side of the grader to see what had invaded his territory.

"Holy shit!" Devin practically dove into her lap in his effort to get out the door on her side. His abrupt exit had including popping the clutch and stomping on the brake. The engine stalled and the grader lurched, tumbling him out into a windrow of freshly scraped soil.

Tiffany couldn't help herself. The laugh started somewhere deep and simply burst out of her. She couldn't remember the last time she'd laughed.

"Oh, you should see yourself, Devin."

"What the hell was that?" He was scanning the sky from where he lay in the dirt as if the zombie apocalypse was about to land on him.

"A bald eagle. Jake is more show than substance. He only fledged last year. Bald eagles take a while before they become majestic."

Jake decided they were of no interest and caught a thermal to climb up above the ridge.

"He's harmless if you're bigger than a salmon," she reassured Devin who still hadn't moved.

"Am I bigger than a salmon?"

"Most of them," Tiffany managed to keep her voice normal as she told the fib.

# # #

Devin slowly climbed to his feet, leaving his dignity in the dirt.

Tiffany sat in the cab as if ready to drive the machine herself. Probably could, and better than the mess he was making of it.

"I thought it was a dragon right out of myth and fable. I've never seen one before and definitely not that close. They don't look so big in documentaries." He squinted up at the sky, but the eagle was now little more than a black dot.

"They look small on the backs of coins, too."

That made Devin smile. Ms. Forthright. "Right. The ones on the backs of coins must be a very small breed. Maybe they should put moths on the backs of quarters; they would fit better."

"Moths are lousy at looking noble. Perhaps we need bigger coins."

"Life-size currency? You'd need one of these," he kicked the grader's tire, "to carry it around."

"Graders don't carry things. They scrape things."

That stopped him. She was speaking perfectly seriously. Again that simple woman showed through the fancifully complex one.

"I think I've got this thing figured out now, if I could arrange for eagles to not interrupt my train of thought." He circled around and climbed back in the other side of the cab so that he didn't have to crawl over her lap again. The smell of her was overwhelming as he sat once more beside her. In a world of dirt and a hint of motor oil, she was like a fresh breeze. His train of thought was headed in a direction that had nothing to do with this machine.

"If so, show me."

He almost took her command as an order to kiss her, but caught himself at the last moment and turned back to the controls.

# # #

He'd finished the meadow and cut the road. Tiffany was no more sure than he was about how to cut ditches and widen turns, but between them, they figured it out. When it was all done, he drove out to the lighthouse and parked the road grader with its nose pointing toward the sea. The engine turned over a few final, thudding times after he'd shut it down, then there was only the pinging of hot metal and the ringing in his ears.

Again, the infinite expanse of water spread before him. As his hearing recovered, the low roar of the ocean filled in the background. Then Tiffany's soft breathing in the foreground.

He turned to face her and they were nearly nose to nose.

"Well done," her voice was a whisper of praise that felt greater than any he'd received before.

"I couldn't have done it alone," which was true. She'd pushed him to learn and to be better than he thought he was.

She shrugged as if dismissing the compliment.

"No, really," he raised a hand to her cheek when she tried to turn away. His fingers buzzed from the strong vibrations of handling the big machine all morning. But through his fingertips he could feel the impossible softness of her skin. Her thick hair slid across the back of his hand like cool water soothing a hot day.

Then he leaned in and kissed her.

There was a muffled sound of surprise, but she didn't pull away or push at him. For a long moment they held the kiss, his whirling thoughts stilled by the soft warmth and the simple acceptance.

Then between one eye blink and the next, she was gone. Out of the cab, on the ground, and moving away.

He scrambled after her before she could do her disappearing act again. "Tiffany! I—"

"Don't!" She commanded him to silence, but at least she stopped her hell-bent retreat a single step from the edge of the forest. Standing with her back to him and her head down, she stood still for a long time before turning. It was hard waiting, but he knew it was the right thing to do.

When she did turn, her hair covered much of her face, but he could feel as much as see her steady gaze upon him. There was no sign of the seemingly simple, overly direct woman now.

"I—" he tried again, but she held up a hand to stop him.

"What were you thinking?" She didn't make it an accusation, rather a literal question.

"I wasn't," but that wasn't a sufficient answer. "I was thinking how kind you are to help me learn that thing," he waved a hand back at the grader. "And how heady a mixture it is to find someone so beautiful yet so powerful."

"So you took me out parking on Lover's Lane in a Cat 112F road grader, hoping for second base or a home run?" There was a dead flatness to her tone.

"No, I—" then he turned to look at the grader. This would be an ideal spot for lovers. In fact, he should install a couple of park benches for guests who wanted to sit together and admire the view. Just there, with concrete pads so that it would last. He mentally rearranged the parking lot for the cottage to make a couple of spaces to park facing the view just as the road grader now stood. "No. I didn't kiss you for that reason."

He turned to see her reaction, but was alone in the midst of the scraped-smooth meadow. Tiffany had stepped beneath the trees and had almost faded away completely.

He took a step into the cool shade to follow her, but stopped after that single step. She had changed in the woods.

She now held a vicious looking bow, nearly as tall as she was, with a half dozen arrows in a holder built onto the frame. It was complex, painted in camouflage forest colors, and looked dangerous as hell.

"You really know how to use that thing?"

In answer, she pulled an arrow from holder to string in a smooth, practiced motion. Faster than he could follow, she drew, aimed, and let fly. The arrow whistled dangerously as it passed over his shoulder.

He turned to follow its flight.

It struck a tree on the far side of the meadow, close beside the grader. It made an audible *Thwap!* where it stuck hard and vibrated. He definitely was no longer in Chicago.

"Uh, I'll remember not to upset you while you have that. I kissed you because you are—"

He turned back, but she was gone. In that single moment she had slipped away as if she'd never been there at all.

"—so amazing." He told the listening forest.

When it didn't answer, he stepped back into the meadow. He would respect her privacy and not go looking for her.

Especially not when she was armed with that bow.

Only two things proved that he hadn't lost his mind and hallucinated her. A line of woman-sized boot prints upon the pristine soil from the grader to the forest. And an arrow driven into the heart of a tree.

Chapter 3

T*iffany was tired of* running away. It seemed as if she'd been doing it her whole life prior to Eagle Cove. And now she was doing it here.

Devin's kiss had been…lovely. She'd spent much of the night trying to find another word for it, but had been unable to.

For a long moment she'd given in, aware only of the lovely kiss. Then she'd snapped out of it as if slapped. Next would come grope, pin, and take! She wasn't going to go there again. Wasn't going to let some man have his way with her against her consent ever again.

Yet Devin's kiss had been…lovely.

Great-gran Lillian's journal didn't help matters either. When needing advice, Tiffany had taken to opening it at random and reading whatever passage presented itself.

March 1900

Ernest is a common sailor, who has just delivered fresh news from San Francisco. My daughter's business efforts on our behalf continue well.

Unknowingly, she has given me the greatest gift when she chose him as the messenger. He may be an unlettered man, but he is wonderfully handsome and such hands he has.

When he unlaced my corset and scooped his rough palms over the most private areas of my bare torso, it was but the beginning of what I discovered that my poor Clarence could never give me while he still lived.

Tiffany slapped the journal closed. She did not need the romance portion of Lillian's long journal. The next weeks of entries, Tiffany knew, would read like the best steamy romance novel, filled with tantalizing snippets and moments. Clarence, the good man, had provided home, daughter, and been a fumbler in bed. Ernest had been the handsome lover who came to her when she was a lonely woman of forty—while her daughter celebrated her twentieth year in San Francisco.

"I'm losing my mind," she'd told Fitz, who hadn't argued the point.

Neither had Tall Guy nor the goats.

But she wasn't going to run any more.

So, when it was time to head down into town for the Tuesday knitting group, she didn't shy off. She also didn't take the path that could have avoided the cottage clearing.

"I'll just wave politely and continue down the road. I'm mature enough to do that." A part of her wanted to take the bow and arrows in case Devin became unruly, but she hid it in the usual spot.

No Devin to be seen. Tire tracks marked the departing grader but no other sign. Nor was there any vehicle parked at the "Lover's Lane" spot beside the lighthouse. Instead there was only the cottage and a half acre of unblemished earth. It would need a flower garden and perhaps an herb garden to make it homey. The arrow that Devin had left in the tree would definitely have to go. Though it was nice that he'd left it in place. He'd probably forgotten about it the moment she was gone… but some part of her knew that wasn't true. He might even be upset if she took it down.

When she turned to leave the barely recognizable meadow, the road was another harsh shock. Other than the occasional US Coast Guard four-by-four truck sent up to inspect the lighthouse, no one else had tried to get a vehicle up here in the three years she'd lived in the State of Tiffany.

Now there was a clear passage down the lower part of the hill. Where there had been a gentle forest trail, there was now a wide and civilized dirt road. It was hard to not think about its surface. She could see each place she had made an adjustment to the cut of the blade. Could remember how it felt to be rubbing shoulders with Devin as they jounced over patches that were still rough in the early passes.

Devin had been so comfortable. Why did he have to ruin it with—

Though maybe she shouldn't lay all of the blame on him. He'd done nothing beyond a simple kiss. She had been the one to over-react. Yet another thing she didn't like about yesterday's memory.

"What are you thinking about so seriously?"

Tiffany was jolted to realize that she'd exited the trees and arrived at the Lamont B&B without first checking to see who might be there. And now that she did, the first thing she noticed was that Devin's truck wasn't here either.

But Gina Lamont was and she had her knitting bag draped over her shoulder.

"Hello, Gina. I'm sorry. My mind was wandering."

They climbed into Gina's Prius together. When Tuesday afternoon knitting had moved from the B&B out to Becky's

Brewery near the airport, Gina Lamont had offered her a ride. Her first time in a car in years, it had been bewildering—as confusing as the unexpected kindness. Now she was used to the feel of her typical two-mile walk between the B&B and town sliding by in mere minutes. And Gina extended her kindness to Tiffany every week as if it was a simple "of course" assumption with no idea how rare and precious that was.

As rare and precious as a kiss.

"You're doing that thinking thing again," Gina told her as they turned onto Beach Way. "About something juicy, I hope."

Not a chance that Tiffany was going to answer that. Instead, she watched the stores go by: Merganser Weaving and Fishing Tours, Carrier Pigeon Pizza (that didn't deliver), Blackbird Bakery (that did), Brass Plover Inn, and Puffin Bay Diner anchored at the far end of town close by the water.

Gina didn't push, and for that alone she deserved an answer.

"I'm just being startled by all of the changes happening."

"Like the lighthouse cottage project?"

"And the road. And your and Natalya's weddings."

"What's wrong with those?" Gina sounded suddenly defensive.

"Nothing. That's not it." Tiffany floundered. "It's not what I meant." She tried again. "Your weddings were so beautiful and you all looked so happy. I just…" And she finally ran out of words.

"And you started thinking about your own."

"Right. What? No!"

Gina's big laugh filled the car. "I know. I watched Monica remarry Ralph for the fourth time and I didn't think much of it. But when Peggy married, that was a shock to the core. She and I had been single-type girls together since forever. And there she suddenly was, wearing wedding white and looking as if she owned the world. What woman wouldn't want that feeling?"

This one, Tiffany thought. But it didn't sit well.

"And I can tell you what's even crazier," Gina said as they parked in front of the old cow barn that was now Becky Billings BlueBird Brewery. "It's completely true."

"For you," Tiffany hadn't meant to make it sound like an accusation.

"I dare you to ask Jessica and Becky about that during knitting. Natalya too, if she wasn't away on her honeymoon."

Tiffany shook her head. That was a dare she wouldn't be taking.

Gina's laugh led them out of the car and indoors to join the knitting circle.

# # #

Devin surveyed the airstrip and couldn't help but feel good about it.

He'd driven the road grader back through town this morning, with a minimum of mishaps, though he'd had to stop and pull a parking sign back into position, mostly, at Kingfisher's Court, and had gotten lost again among the seabird roads—they wound and twisted and overlapped as if they were in flight themselves.

He'd started talking advanced grader technique with Peggy, which had turned into a long discussion. Then she'd sent him out to scrape and shape the runway. With her instructions in his head, he'd finally gotten a good feel for the machine and had enjoyed refinishing the runway's surface before she returned from another flight.

"Nice job," she said after landing her Stearman 4 biplane and taxiing back and forth over the surface a few times. "Can I borrow you for a minute more? I have to carry a couple of pies over to Becky's." She nodded toward a barn across a hundred yards of pasture deep in hay.

"It might cost you a slice," Devin warned.

Peggy nodded at the deal.

"What do I owe you for the grader?"

"Nothing. Gina lends me a room whenever my sister comes to visit—which I count as a blessing because she makes me too crazy to have close night and day. Besides, I'll consider the nice job on the runway as me owing you."

Devin sniffed at the pie she placed in his hands. He did it again, deeper. Strawberry-rhubarb. Not a construction man worth his salt wasn't an expert on pies.

He was also getting the hang of how things worked away from the city.

"Smells like a slice of this will set us even there. If it tastes even half as good as it smells, I'll owe you."

"Good," Peggy picked up another pie and a cloth bag in which he could see some yarn and needles. "Because it tastes even better."

There was a narrow path beaten through the hay, which was waist high. Chicago snow had just been melting out at his non-wedding. By the time he'd left a month later to drive west, the hay fields were barely ankle high. They had some kind of crazy growing season out here on the coast. When was everything going to stop surprising him?

Not yet!

That question was answered soundly when he stepped through the barn's side door. He'd seen the "5B—Becky Billings BlueBird Brewery Tasting Room" sign and assumed it was some hobby operation. He remembered the short blonde who had danced in the darkness with her husband after the wedding. He expected a little craft setup.

Through the tasting room door was a spacious area with a dozen tables and a long bar sporting a dozen taps. It was a beautiful space that made him want to sit down and draw a pint.

Up above the bar was a painting of Eagle Cove as it would appear from Peggy's plane, reaching from wall to wall and from bar mirror to peaked ceiling.

"Your photo originally?"

Peggy nodded.

The representation of the town itself looked modern and had been painted by an artist who managed to bring the high view to life. Another artist had painted framing images of an old-time sailing ship and a couple of women in Victorian garb.

"Don't miss this," Peggy called his attention to a long glass wall beyond which stood an immaculate brewery. "I helped Becky assemble most of this. Her work, I was just labor." She didn't need to mention how proud of it she was; it was clear in her voice.

Tall, stainless steel tanks surrounded a big copper kettle and a host of other mysterious equipment. There was one person in back working a bottling machine. The guy waved and Peggy nodded back, her hands full of pie.

Peggy led Devin into a big living room area. A dozen women were gathered in a big circle, chatting happily. There seemed to be three or four conversations going at once and he estimated that his best strategy was to grab a slice and beat a hasty retreat.

Calls of greetings sounded out for Peggy, and then one by one the conversations quieted as heads turned, noticing him for the first time. He'd met Gina, Mrs. Winslow, Jessica, and Becky. He recognized several others from the wedding even if he hadn't met them.

Maybe he'd skip the slice and just beat a hasty retreat.

That was the plan until a person sitting on one end of a couch turned slowly to look in his direction.

Tiffany Mills' hands stopped with their knitting, even as the rest of the room resumed what they were doing. Was there anything she couldn't do? Play harp, knit, farm, and shoot a bow and arrow.

That image had cost him an entire night's sleep.

Tiffany with her feet well planted in the forest, her long hair billowing soft in the breeze, and smoothly powerful in her handling of the bow. Robin Hood would be an idiot if he didn't recruit Maid Tiffany after a single glance. Forget Marian, whether played by Olivia de Havilland, Mary Elizabeth Mastrantonio, or even Cate Blanchett (his personal favorite—true of almost any movie Cate was in). Tiffany wielding her bow and arrow was a revelation.

Peggy took the pie from his hands. "Sit while I slice these up."

Devin headed for the seat over by the brewery's master control board. At least that's what he hoped it was, because if there was another one with even more controls and readouts he didn't want to know about it. These controls were plenty complex enough.

"Don't disappoint me," Peggy's whisper was sharp and private.

Devin looked at her and again was the target of her steady gaze. "I'm not blind, so don't you be stupid."

Which was exactly what he'd been about to do. Sure he was curious to see what information a brewery reported to its operator. But there was also an empty chair close beside the couch Tiffany was seated on. "For a slice, I'll sit for a bit," he offered loudly enough to be heard.

Peggy rolled her eyes at him, but nodded when he turned for the chair by Tiffany.

Devin had three steps to figure out how to approach this.

Only a pissant would embarrass her in front of her friends.

He could act hurt that she'd bolted.

Or he could pretend everything was normal, as if their last conversation had merely been interrupted.

He sat, smiled at her, and looked down at her knitting. "Wow!"

He'd never seen anything like it. Intricate designs in multi-colored yarns made beautiful pictures creating a tube that he could only imagine would be a scarf someday. A glance revealed that it was easily the most complex piece in the room. He turned back quickly so that she wouldn't disappear.

"What's that?" He nodded down to her knitting.

# # #

Tiffany looked down at it and she had absolutely no idea.

Devin's unexpected arrival had broken the seams of normality she kept wrapped around herself during knitting.

"It's—" It had been so clear in her head just seconds ago, but like a dropped stitch, it was gone without noticing.

Devin leaned in and traced a finger over one of the patterns.

It felt as if his finger traced upon her cheek, just where he'd touched her before the kiss.

"It looks like a windmill."

"It is," Tiffany gasped out. She remembered that now, the long propellers of a big windfarm on a field of dark blue. "Denmark. Copenhagen. The water is so shallow that they plant them in the bay like giant tulips."

"Have you been there?"

She shook her head. "But I've seen pictures of them standing in the sea." Her family had traveled a lot, but mostly to the Orient, where her stepfather's business interests had been. "This is my anti-trip."

"Anti-trip?" Devin's finger traced over other patterns. "Places you've never been but want to go?"

That had Tiffany looking up at him in surprise. "Yes. Exactly."

"What are the green steps?"

"Vineyard terraces of Liguria."

"And this?"

"Gelato, by the cone and cup."

Devin had her lead him through her fanciful adventure, a bit of Scottish tartan, a classic Fair Isle pattern from the Shetlands and another from the Highlands. It was actually a map of her heritage: Scottish, Italian, a little Norse, and a chambermaid of Henry VIII (at least according to family legend), who'd been banished to Alnwick Castle for producing yet another girl for the king without a male heir. Online, Tiffany had found water sculptures in the Alnwick gardens and included those for the chambermaid.

"F," she explained on the last section he pointed to, a whole row of them connected together in a long chain: black with white block letters. "For Fitzinger the cat."

"The orca-colored cat."

He'd remembered. She wasn't sure if she was charmed or if it felt a little intrusive.

"Why Fitzinger?"

"Leopold Fitzinger was the first to include the killer whale in a genus-species taxonomy."

His laugh tipped her over into charmed.

It was easy to join in.

Then she was aware of the abrupt silence around the entire circle of women. It was as if her and Devin's shared laughter had snipped off all other threads of conversation. A quick peek revealed that, indeed, everyone was looking in their direction with differing reactions. Jessica was scowling at Devin, Becky and Gina were both smiling as if to say "of course." Most were simply surprised. Maggie Winslow looked at her thoughtfully—not at Devin, at her.

Tiffany tried to read her expression, but it was elusive. Neither surprise nor misconceived congratulations, but rather as if she was somehow finding Tiffany's laugh as food for thoughts of her own.

Unable to stand the pressure, she shot to her feet, barely rescued her knitting, and headed out the door.

Devin caught up with her a dozen steps across the gravel parking lot.

"I'm sorry. You should go back with your friends. I'll leave. I'm sorry for making you uncomfortable."

She shook her head, then tried to explain. "It's not you that's making me uncomfortable."

Devin blinked at her several times and then offered one of those glorious smiles she was rapidly learning to appreciate. "Let me guess: that's exactly what *is* making you uncomfortable. That you aren't uncomfortable around me."

"I—" she shrugged. "No point in denying that, since you're right. You don't have to look so pleased." And he did look terribly happy with his discovery.

"Do you want to go back?"

Tiffany considered the closed door. Her friends were in there. Actual friends. Ones concerned for her and ones happy for her.

Actual, real, live people she would count as friends. Then she looked back at Devin. She thought about his kiss and the way his questions about her knitting had tickled up her spine. And oddly, about the arrow he'd left in the tree like some lucky talisman.

Devin waited patiently while she dragged her thoughts back from the four winds.

"I—" She was going to have to find a way to start sentences without stuttering to a stop every time. "I," she pushed through, "would rather spend some time with you." There, she'd said it. Not what she'd expected to say, but still it was true.

He offered one of his great smiles, "I know this great parking spot."

She heard the tease this time and the flirt.

"Hang on," he raised a finger, then turned to the brewery and went back inside.

Tiffany was left to stand in the gravel parking lot, reviewing the conversation to see where it had gone astray. He'd left her to go and…do what?

"We can't miss these," Devin came back out carefully balancing two paper plates, each with a generous slice of pie.

"We'll need forks."

"Crap! Here," he handed her the pie plates so quickly she almost lost them to the gravel drive. Then he ducked back inside and returned wielding two plastic forks. "I had to promise a day of labor in the brewery if I don't return these. I think Becky was kidding." He took back one of the pie slices and then nodded across the hay field toward the hangar.

She could see his little pickup parked there and followed him to it.

It was a totally different experience riding through town in Devin's small truck than Gina's Prius. And it wasn't just the additional height off the road. The last time she'd been in a car with a man had been her assistant three years ago who helped her start the farm. Now a man was driving and she felt as if she was floating. But she was also conscious of the closeness. The

SR5 was not a big truck and it felt closed in. Not unsafe, just… as if a pressure was squeezing her gently inward like a dive into deep water.

"Don't lose our pie," Devin's admonition grounded her in the moment.

She held the two plates, one balanced on either knee. They were perfectly safe, why was he—

"I mean, who knows if we can trust the guy who cut this road." Again he made it easy to smile at his joke.

Tiffany had daydreamed herself all the way to the B&B. Devin didn't stop. He rolled out the far side of the little parking lot by the big Victorian and turned up the hill along his newly cut road.

He needn't have worried. The surface was smooth and well packed; his truck climbed it easily.

Rather than parking alongside the lighthouse and facing outward as he had with the road grader, he turned and backed the truck into the same place. Tiffany was now looking toward her path home—across the newly shorn and level meadow and off into the trees. She felt no desire to run this time, but didn't know what Devin was doing. The view was now behind her.

He came around and opened her door as if she was some sort of a lady. "I'll take those," and he lifted away the two pie plates.

Now what was she supposed to do? *Get out of the truck for one thing, Tiffany.* And when she did, she saw that Devin had lowered the tailgate and perched on it facing the ocean. The evening sun was ducking down into the clouds far out to sea, lighting up the sky with warm yellows and soft oranges. The sea was calm; the breakers down below no more than five or six feet high where they crashed into the rocks at the base of Orca Head. The ocean breeze was still warm in the sun, though it would be cool in the shade.

It was cooler here; the tailgate put her at more ease than the close confines of the truck's cab. Somehow Devin had known that. She scooted up next to him and he handed her a slice of pie. They ate together in a comfortable silence and watched the sun's slow progress down into the clouds holding just offshore.

"Good pie," she said when the silence had stretched long enough.

"I carried it from Peggy's myself."

"Tough job."

"Glad to do it." Again the silence sat with them for a few minutes before the breeze brushed it away. "So, tell me about your anti-trip. I've never really traveled much outside Chicago."

"My stepfather always took us to the Orient. I speak Japanese and Mandarin…but neither has ever felt right, like my brain and my mouth weren't built for those sounds. I heard a tape of Gaelic and somehow it made sense. It's a crazy language, but it simply fit."

"Which language is hardest? I only speak English and construction-crew Spanish, which isn't presentable anywhere except a build site."

"It depends…" and Tiffany marveled at herself as they discussed language and the travels they each hadn't done. She hadn't understood until this moment how little she'd spoken to men over the last few years. It was as if she'd forgotten how, had fallen out of practice. But Devin made it easy to recall, like a long forgotten sweater that still fit once patched, both familiar and new.

When they finished their pie, Devin tossed the paper plates into the back of his truck, but tucked the plastic forks safely into a pocket and winked at her. Then he continued telling her about his cross-country road trip and how that had made him realize what he'd been missing by staying anchored in Chicago.

If it had been a long time since she'd talked to a man, it had been even longer since she'd kissed one. She didn't really count yesterday's brief kiss. It had been ninety percent alarm on her part and only about ten percent kiss.

"I know I have to go back to Chicago at some point, but for now—"

For now.

Now!

Tiffany grabbed her nerves, wrestled them into submission, then leaned over and kissed Devin. She caught him mid-word, which should have been awkward, but he didn't let it be.

He tasted of strawberry-rhubarb pie.

When he slid an arm about her shoulders and held her close, she didn't feel trapped at all. Instead she was whirled up into a maelstrom of feelings. Her heart was moving blood at an unheard of rate, so fast the sonic boom was making her ears ring. She felt as if she could step off the cliff edge and fly over the sea as long as—

Devin pulled back first and she almost fell forward off the tailgate at the aftershock. She'd never so thrown herself at man in her life. But before embarrassment or confusion could take hold, Devin whispered softly.

"Hot damn!"

"Hot damn?" Tiffany was amazed that she could speak.

"Well, it sounds more western than 'Holy Shit!' or 'Son of a Bitch!' which would be more common in Chicago."

"Properly I'd be 'Daughter of a Bitch!' Which has the advantage of being true."

"Maybe we should introduce our moms. Sounds as if they'd hit it off."

Tiffany's head was still spinning. Moms, amazing kisses, and throwing herself at Devin all collided to leave her speechless. Deep inside she decided that she definitely agreed with his assessment on one point though: *Hot damn!*

"If I'd ever met a woman who kissed like that…" Devin left her hanging for a long moment as he stared out to sea. "I guess I'd never have come to Eagle Cove."

It sounded as if he was speaking to himself, but she couldn't feel guilty for eavesdropping. Then he turned back to her, cupped her cheek in his callused palm, and kissed her lightly. This time all rational thought didn't tumble down to plunge into the sea, but there was still a dreamy sense of rightness as she pressed her own palm in turn upon his cheek. There was an impossible rightness to it.

Maybe now she understood better the long sections of Lillian's journal where she had waxed eloquent upon how a man made her feel. But Tiffany didn't want to use her ancestor's words—this was her time. Her moment.

"Kissing you," she whispered against Devin's lips, "feels as right as speaking Gaelic."

# # #

"We've had the dessert portion of our evening." Devin was unwilling to let her go yet but they couldn't spend the whole evening sitting on the back of his pickup truck. The wind was picking up and it was turning chilly.

"And the kissing portion," Tiffany agreed.

"Now it must be time for the movie portion," Devin agreed, happily quoting one of the funniest movies ever. "I can't believe you know *My Favorite Year.*"

"The problem is, did you see what's playing at The Flicker? *The Poseidon Adventure.* The 2005 version."

"Ack, gack!" Devin grabbed his throat and made choking noises until Tiffany laughed. Then he remembered Peggy had told him about Greg Slater's Tuesday night for locals and that he qualified. He grabbed Tiffany's hand and dragged her around to the passenger door of his truck.

"What? Where are we going?"

"I think it's time for the dinner portion of the evening, don't you?"

"No! Wait!"

But he knew if he waited, she'd slip away again. He closed the truck door, reached in through the open window, and toggled the lock. Then he rested his hands on the door frame and hoped as hard as he could.

She only would have to move her finger a few inches to unlock the door. And he would open it and let her go if she did. Slowly, ever so slowly, she turned to look up at him. She gazed a long time into his eyes. Then with a soft smile and that same impossibly slow action, Tiffany reached out and took hold of the seatbelt.

Devin held onto the door and hung his head until he heard the soft click of it engaging. He didn't know why it took so much out of him or why he hoped so hard, but it had and he did.

He climbed in beside her and drove them slowly back into town.

# # #

Tiffany hadn't eaten in a restaurant in three years. And not in a high-end one since leaving San Francisco most of a decade ago.

Greg had transformed The Puffin. Fluorescent lighting had been abandoned and replaced by twinkle lights and table candles. Sheers had been drawn across the big windows, not quite hiding the main street, but softening it, making it feel far away. Worn Formica was masked by midnight blue table cloths. The individual tables had been pushed into a long line for communal service.

It was in some sort of dreamlike fugue that Tiffany floated through the evening. It became a scattershot of images. Greg's delight at her arrival. He and Devin debating about paying for the meal—Devin had ended up jamming two twenty-dollar bills down the back of Greg's pants when he'd turned away thinking he'd won. When Greg had dug them out and tried to give them back, Devin had raised his palms outward. "Eww!"

Tiffany had mimicked the motion and they had all three laughed together.

She knew many of the people who came; they greeted her as if nothing was out of the ordinary. Greg had seated them at one end and she recognized but didn't know the couple beside them, which was perfect. Mrs. Winslow and Hector at the far end—paying such attention to each other than Tiffany almost wondered if Mrs. Winslow hadn't seen her. She'd certainly made no fuss.

The food was exquisite. Her leeks showed up in the onion soup. The beets had been sliced, roasted to sweetness, and topped with a chilled salad based on fresh-caught crab. Snow peas adorned Asian-spiced rockfish. Fresh-made strawberry gelato with a dark chocolate sauce finished the meal. Becky's beers had accompanied each course in tiny taster glasses that matched to perfection.

There was only one thing in the entire meal that didn't blur together until she couldn't separate one thing from another.

Devin.

They talked movies, books, and even plays. It all meant nothing, and it all meant everything. Not once did he ask about her past, her farm, or even about her. Yet between their meaningless words, she was unsure if she had ever told anyone so much about herself.

# # #

The sun had turned the sky red-gold and the sea black by the time he drove Tiffany back to the lighthouse meadow. At the invisible trailhead—Devin had assumed it was just a rabbit track when he'd scouted the edge of the woods two days before, looking for where she'd gone—she turned to him.

No words.

She simply placed a warm hand on the center of his chest, as if keeping him carefully away for a moment. He reached up with both hands to catch her thick hair and brush it back over her shoulders. He wanted a clear view of her face despite the fading light. Her fine lips and strong eyebrows came from her father's Scots heritage, or so she'd said. The slender oval of her face from Italy. The hair and the shy smile, those were completely hers.

Rather than kissing him, she shifted her hand around his waist and hugged him. Hard.

There was no hesitation. No worries that he might "muss up" the woman in his arms. She simply held onto him and he did the same to her.

The crazy synergy of their kiss slammed back in, then built at a steamroller pace. When Tiffany hugged him, nothing was held in reserve. He could feel the soft curves of her body pressing against his as well as the fierce strength of her arms wrapped about his waist. When she rested her head on his shoulder, all he could think about was never letting go.

And then with a smile and a softly-whispered "Thank you," she slipped away into the dark forest. Just mere steps into the trees and she was gone like a ghost.

Chapter 4

W*ednesday was delivery day* and Tiffany spent much of it running her ATV with its little trailer out through the woods. She had a deal with a farm supply over in Eugene for biweekly deliveries of goat and chicken feed, along with anything else she called in. Once her garden had started producing and she'd canned a season's worth of food, her personal needs had been minimal. They also delivered propane whenever the biweekly truck driver noticed it was running low.

Her pick-up point was two miles up an old logging road that had the advantage of meeting the highway well out of town. The driver always dropped the load in a lean-to she'd placed along that road. It was the closest any vehicle bigger than an ATV could travel.

Three years before, after finishing with the heavy equipment, she'd planted a thick patch of native trees across the end of where her access driveway had been. In just a few months they'd blended into the forest until there was no sign that there had ever been a turn-off onto this road lost deep in the woods. A hundred feet before her now-hidden driveway, she'd built the lean-to mostly out of moss-covered logs and branches from the forest floor and topped it with rusted, corrugated metal. It had looked thirty years abandoned by the time it was done—exactly the effect she was after. On the back side, where it couldn't be seen without knowing it was there, stood her propane tank. After each delivery, she used a rake to spread forest floor detritus over her fresh tracks.

The lean-to also kept the feedbags and other supplies dry while waiting for her to fetch them in the thin rain that had moved in overnight. She'd heard it patter on the yurt's roof as she lay awake and considered the effects of her choices.

Three years alone in the woods had definitely been the best years of her life…so far. It was the "so far" that kept niggling at her, like a mischievous angel poking at her with a terribly ticklish feather—a very uncomfortable feeling. For the first time in a long while, a part of her had awoken with a question, a new one.

"What's next?"

She had no clearer idea after she'd pulled on slicks and tromped out into the morning weather.

Rain wasn't a constant on the coast like most people thought; instead it was a whimsical force that often slid in from the ocean with little warning. More often than long steady pours, it arrived as brutal dumps, then moved on. Her rain gauge had counted sixty-five inches last year (three-point-two inches in one day was her record so far) and this year was right on track—January had been chilly and dry, but February had already more than made up for it in sheeting downpours. March had again been dry and surprisingly warm. Only time would tell what April would provide. Her Wednesday delivery day was a "typical" long, slow drizzle, just heavy enough to require she wear slicks and just warm enough that she cooked in them.

She spent most of Thursday, after the storm system had thankfully moved inland and left behind a patchy gray overcast, shifting the goat pen. It was a challenging task as the goats were always so glad to see her that she could barely move as they clustered around. Maybe letting them learn that she always had some treat in her pockets had been a mistake. She doled out bits of early carrot and kale. Why in the world she'd ever planted kale she didn't know. It was healthy, but tough and took forever to cook.

Tiffany didn't mind the crowding. The baby goats were calf-high and bounced about as if their legs were made of pogo sticks. She was out of names from *Little Women*. She considered *Star Trek*, but if she did, she'd run out after Uhura and Chapel and have to name them all for Kirk's women. This year's kids would be from *Fiddler on the Roof*. Soon Tzeitel, Hodel, and Chava were all chasing Motel Kamzoil around the pen. If the last two were girls, they'd be Shprintze and Bielke; all five girls together again.

She'd brought a couple of biscuits for Tall Guy, who she then teased about how she'd met another man. He'd nodded his big black muzzle and huffed out a sigh as if that was only to be expected, or perhaps because she'd only brought two biscuits.

Devin was never far from her thoughts. There seemed to be an amplitude curve—the closer she worked to the west end of her property where the trail led to the lighthouse, the more aware of him she became. That's part of why she was working on the goat pen to the east. She wasn't exactly avoiding him, but she wasn't seeking him out either. That the pen needed moving—well, almost—was only part of the excuse.

Tiffany discovered that it was confusing to be attracted to a man again. It was as if that part of her had fallen so out of practice that the signals were constantly crossing. Social graces had never been one of her strengths but she'd gone out with a few nice guys in college and grad school, and "few" had been just fine with her. But with three years alone in the woods, she'd lost what little skills she'd had.

Lunging at Devin when she'd wanted to kiss him…the memory made her wince at her own ineptness. A woman was supposed to be…what?

"Well for one thing," she told Beth, who had always been her favorite goat, a dainty gray with black boots and a white mask, "she's not supposed to smell like a goat unless she is one." Amy came over—all elegant in her pure, soft silver coat—because she always did when another goat was receiving attention. Tiffany knew that she wouldn't smell of goat, she'd reek of it. She gave in and sat upon the drying grass to play with them and rest from the heavy work of moving the fence. Tall Guy took that as an invitation to come over and sit on her lap to keep her firmly in place.

"At a hundred and thirty pounds, you are not a lap dog," she groaned.

In answer, he began beating her in the ribs with wags of his great tail.

"A woman isn't supposed to smell like a dog either," but she scratched his ear as he kept her pinned to the wet grass.

Another happy thump against her ribs.

"I guess dog is better than goat."

As if she had a choice.

Was there anything else she could do to be *less* attractive to her own species?

# # #

Devin walked into the Puffin Bay Diner as it opened on Friday morning—and was nearly bowled over by Cal Sr. coming in on his heels.

"I swear. This is the last time Junior ever gets to leave town on a honeymoon. That's it. One time only." Cal stormed up to the counter and called out to the Judge working over his grill. "Tall stack, John. And double up on the coffee, Greg," he told the waiter, a slender man who might be the retired judge's son.

"Trouble at the bakery?" Greg poured him a mug.

"Wasn't paying enough attention these last few years. Junior has made all of these little expansions to our business, and dealt with 'em just fine without me really noticing. Now I'm making beer bread for the brewery, sourdough for our lunch service, pizza dough for Carrier Pigeon. Damn list goes on forever. And now Vincent McCall comes in wanting some kind of pretty cake for his tenth anniversary. Damn boy doesn't have a clue what, which tells me that Dawn didn't send him because she'd have included instructions—guess he's finally thinking how to keep her happy, but now it's making me *unhappy* as I can't just call up the girl and ask what she wants."

"Do you have their wedding cake on file?" Mrs. Winslow asked from where she'd come in behind Devin. "Pineapple Upside Down Cake if I recall. A single tier, as they were very poor when they started out. I suggest that you add a second tier as a marker of their success in building a family."

"Great! Thanks, Maggie. You're a wonder and that's the truth."

"Tell that to my students. Are you planning to stand there all day, boy?" She said the last to Devin.

"Uh, no, ma'am." Devin got caught between a smile that she must be hell on her second graders and a wince at the admonition aimed his way. She waved him to one of the tables and, like a bad little boy, he headed for his corner.

The Puffin Bay Diner was a classic diner plucked right out of the fifties. Worn linoleum flooring. A dozen battered Formica tables of indeterminate color. Fresh paint and a mixture of art on the walls. There were two main artists represented, and the work was exceptional by both. They were almost related, but the vision was so different that they had to be two people. Even Picasso from Blue to Cubism, as he'd seen at The Art Institute of Chicago, you could see the same hand.

These were somehow the opposite. Here were two very different artists painting with a common emotion in a common theme: a deep love of Eagle Cove. He'd never seen them before, yet the art looked familiar…and then it clicked in. They had joined their talents to paint the big mural in Becky Billings BlueBird Brewery.

He'd never been an art collector, that was one of his mother's things. She'd buy exceptional pieces of art and then loan them to the Art Institute as long as they were prominently labeled with "On Loan from the Private Collection of…" But he might have to buy one of these before he left town. Something to remind him of this place. Maybe a second one to give to his mother as a family peace offering once he was less angry at her. If that ever happened.

Behind him, the big plate glass windows were still dark with the morning. Ahead was a six-stool counter and a big service window back into the kitchen.

Gina had told him last night that someone had called to set up a six a.m. meeting at the diner. She'd declined to say who, though of course she had to know. The women of this town were conspiring to make him crazy.

He'd tried drawing the plans for the renovation up at the lightkeeper's cottage, but it had been wet and chilly these last few days. When he tried to work at the B&B, Gina had hovered. The library, his usual retreat in Chicago, was called the Wolery here (after Owl's home in Winnie the Pooh, the seat of all wisdom in the Hundred Acre Wood), but was only open Tuesdays and Saturdays from two to four.

For something to do, he'd spent most of the last two days ripping out the interior plaster. It had cracked with age. When he'd discovered there was no insulation behind it and the wiring was all turn-of-century (and not the most recent one), there'd been no further question: it had to come down. The problem with straight physical labor was that it left him far too much time to think.

And Tiffany had offered him a kiss and a hug better than any lover, and then evaporated into thin air. No one spoke of her in her absence. No one thought her invisibility was strange. It didn't bother anyone except him, and it was making him completely and totally—

"I thought you might want some help," Mrs. Winslow sat down across the table from him.

"All I'm doing is mucking out at this point, stripping walls and so on." He was currently working under a local contractor's license, a relationship that Gina had arranged with EC Contracting. He hadn't met with the contractor yet—and couldn't read the hieroglyph that passed for the signature of whoever had pulled the permit, except for an N at the start of the last name—but it didn't matter while he was still doing tear-down work. At some point he'd have to meet whoever owned Eagle Cove Contracting and make sure they saw eye to eye on quality and design. He shrugged, "Not that big a job."

Mrs. Winslow stared at him blankly while Greg delivered a menu, only to him.

"Aren't you eating?" Devin didn't want to be the only one eating at the table.

Mrs. Winslow nodded, "My usual if you please, Greg."

Devin stared down at the menu and ordered the first thing he spotted. "Western omelette, but without the onion."

"Nope," the waiter gave him a smile.

"Nope?"

"Nope. You order it and the Judge cooks it however he wants," then he winked. "Hasn't changed the menu in the six years since he retired from judging. Except the waffles, but they're back now."

"Okay," Devin sighed. Who was he kidding? He wasn't going to get another chance to kiss Tiffany again. The way things were going, he'd be glad to just see her again before he left town at the end of the summer. "With the onions is fine. On the side I'd like—"

"Nope," Greg again said with that smile.

"No options there either," Devin could feel his own smile starting up. "Is it okay if I put sugar in my coffee?"

"Sugar in your coffee, yes. You put ketchup on Dad's eggs and you're outta here."

"Deal." Which left him once more facing Dragon Winslow. He'd heard the nickname only the once when Vincent had called her that, but it fit. If he wasn't careful, he'd be saying it aloud.

The bell on the back of the door tinkled.

Dragon Winslow didn't even turn. "Over here, Hector."

"Just let me get my crossword," a tall, spare man in his sixties with thinning silver hair riffled through a copy of *The Oregonian* by the front door and brought one of the sections over to the table.

"Morning, Maggie. Hi," he held out a hand and offered Devin a crushingly powerful grip. "I'm Hector Jackson."

"Yow!" Devin did his best to shift his own grip to take the unexpected squeeze, but he was too little too late. "Devin Robison."

"Heh! Love doing that to young folk," he told the Dragon as he sat down. "Can't let them think that old people are, well, you know, Maggie."

"Old?" Devin offered.

Which earned him a cheerful, silverware rattling thump of agreement from Hector. Dragon Maggie Winslow gave him a chilly look. But he noticed that she offered Hector a smile just a moment later.

"Well, as I was telling…" he hesitated to make sure he chose the proper honorific, "…Mrs. Winslow."

A darting, dark-eyed glance told him that she hadn't missed his hesitation and probably not what was behind it either.

"I'm still tearing out the old interior. The plaster is too brittle and what's behind the walls needs a lot of work."

"Never worked on a house before. Wasn't exactly planning on starting now."

"Then—" Devin stopped in confusion.

"Do you sail, Mr. Robison?"

"Sure, I've been out on Lake Michigan a couple of times in a sailboat. Though usually on my family's—" he bit that off "—power boat." Chicago Master Constructors, Inc. kept their ninety-foot motor yacht for entertaining at the family dock during the summer. In the winter, it was driven out through the Great Lakes and the St. Lawrence Seaway down to the Caribbean for entertaining top clients there. It was the only real travel he'd ever done, hopping the company jet down to the boat, and he hadn't done that in years. Oddly, the Oregon Coast looked far more foreign than a Caribbean island viewed from the sweltering deck of the big yacht.

"Stinkpotter," Hector and the Dragon exchanged smiles.

"What?"

"Boats that need engines aren't boats. They're floating pots that make a stink. It has to have a sail, buddy, or it's not a real boat."

Devin couldn't help but smile as he imagined how his father would react to the slur; he loved his yacht more than his wife, and probably more than his mistress. Thank god these people knew nothing about that connection. There was no more than a shared last name with CMC's CEO to link him with one of the biggest contractors in the Midwest. And at the moment he wished there wasn't even that. D.R. Builders was his own firm, even if he'd left it in his foreman's hands for the summer. He liked it that way.

"I believe that you need to fix that," the Dragon was still talking to Hector.

"Fix what?" Devin had missed something while watching the approach of their breakfasts. He could only goggle at the omelette slid in front of him. It was a four-egger, overflowing with red and green bell pepper, cheese, and sautéed onion. And the sausage and ham in the omelette apparently hadn't been enough meat, because there was a healthy serving of farm patty sausage and hash browns on the side. He wouldn't be hungry for a week if he could even finish this thing.

Dragon Winslow's and Hector's portions were significantly smaller.

"Dad knows that contracting is hungry work," Greg explained. "He also appreciates the runway work you did for his wife."

Devin turned to wave his thanks to the Judge, but only received a level gaze in return. He could imagine Peggy and the Judge trading that exact expression back and forth across the dinner table—mutually unreadable. Except perhaps to each other?

"You're looking at his thanks on the plate." Greg shrugged as if to explain that was typical and was gone again. Devin kept an eye out on the next couple of services as the diner was over half full despite the early hour. His meal was all out of proportion with the still generous servings that were sent out to other tables.

The Dragon was watching him.

"What?" Devin had lost the thread of the conversation.

Hector was the one who answered, but continued talking to the Dragon. "Won the Judge's respect his first week in town. Hard to do."

"Peggy walked Devin's new road above Gina's. She said it was respectably done."

News to Devin.

Then the Dragon turned to face him. "Nine o'clock on Sunday. Be at the docks unless there is no wind."

Devin had been here long enough already to know how unlikely that was. Wind appeared to be one of the constant features of the coast.

Then something shifted in her stern face. The Dragon faded and for the first time he saw deep tenderness that he'd wager she revealed to few.

"I think, young man, that you should bring that girl with you on Sunday. If anyone can coax her off her mountain, I suspect that it is you."

"Sunday?" Devin wondered what possible power he had over Tiffany. Or what strange insight did Mrs. Winslow have that he didn't? "She's invisible. I might not see her before then."

"Oh, I would not worry about that. She never misses Friday knitting. Now, Hector," she picked up her fork, "what is the first clue on your crossword puzzle this morning?"

# # #

Devin spent the early part of Friday afternoon loading debris into his truck so that he wouldn't miss Tiffany's passage down to the B&B for knitting. He was white with plaster dust by the time he was done but he'd seen no sign of her. The tiny nails in the lath strips had caught his clothes and skin, tearing holes in the former and leaving him scratched and scraped. It stung, but it was also comforting in its familiarity. Demolition of plaster was a familiar part of renovating older homes.

He checked the trailhead before leaving for the dump, but there were no new footprints coming out of the woods.

On his way back from the dump, he pulled into the B&B, ostensibly for water and an energy bar, though he had both in his truck. He didn't know how he'd speak to Tiffany in her circle of friends, but he had to at least see her.

In complete contrast to the damp morning, the afternoon was warm, almost hot, and the breeze still. The knitters sat out on the porch. A quick scan—no Tiffany. No empty chair with a pile of elaborate "anti-trip" knitting resting on it, awaiting its mistress' return.

Then Mrs. Winslow looked up from her own knitting and spotted him. With pursed lips, she shook her head ever so slightly. It was impossible to miss the look of concern, which slammed him from cheery to fearful.

He scrambled back to his truck with the barest of courtesies and headed up to the lighthouse. The fact that she was obviously a very capable woman did nothing to turn aside his fear. A bear got her. Or she'd broken a leg and couldn't get up. Or…

Devin slammed the truck to a halt close by the woods. He rummaged among the tools in his truck and grabbed a crowbar for defense before plunging into the woods. After the first dozen paces he was hopelessly entangled in the low, dead branches sticking out from the Douglas fir trees. They broke off easily enough, which said that Tiffany had never passed this way.

He traversed back and forth, looking for some sign. On his third try, he spotted a footprint on a muddy spot among the ferns and branches that littered the forest floor. Once he turned onto the track, he could see a clear passage, but not before. It weaved and veered, but it led in the right general direction for the overlook above the lighthouse meadow.

The shadows jumped at him. A squirrel, far smaller than the big grays of the Chicago parks, chittered at him angrily from where it clung upside-down, far up a tree. Birds scattered away in front of him as if he was hunting them instead of a missing woman. He scanned side to side, at first for signs of Tiffany, then also for signs of bears as he plunged deeper into the woods—he kept his crowbar at the ready.

The forest was bewildering. He'd thought he had a feeling for it from driving through it and working alone at the lighthouse meadow. But nothing prepared him for walking beneath its canopy. The sunlight, almost hot in the still meadow, was a shadowy memory. The occasional glistening shaft would pierce down to illuminate a few square feet of moss, growing on a fallen log, but even that was shadowed by splayed branches. Looking at the sunny spots was a mistake as it darkened the rest of the forest.

Trees soared upward to bewildering heights. The lower branches sported little greenery, leaving bare trunks to reach forever upward. Smaller trees struggled in the darkness. Ferns grew around fallen trees. Some of the fallen had tipped their roots with them, exposing labyrinths of twisted roots and shedding soil two or three times his own height. At one that looked fairly recent, he looked to see if Tiffany lay beside or partly under it. The trunk ran for a hundred feet or more off into the distance; smaller trees were flattened to either side by the blast zone of the giant's crash.

No Tiffany. He hurried on.

He was moving so fast that he almost ran off the cliff at the overlook. It was a narrow ledge over a hundred-foot fall. Not that narrow, but enough to stop him cold. And she passed this way every day?

Devin had walked the ironwork on plenty of his father's skyscrapers but hadn't felt as exposed as he did at this moment. The sweeping hundred-and-eighty-degree view took his breath away and the hundred-foot fall into Terra Incognita nearly took away his nerves. He edged around the curve until he once again picked up the trail.

And now his goal was clearly in sight. A neat area the size of two city blocks had been carved into the wilderness—ten acres or close enough. Much of it was in meadow. But a circular building with a pointed roof was tucked up against the far trees. It was so incongruous that it took him a moment to identify it as a yurt, which he'd only ever seen in photos of the Mongolian nomads. Near it lay a massive garden laid out in neat rows behind a tall fence. There were a few small outbuildings that looked like garages. A large set of solar panels stood on the south slope. The view, he looked over his shoulder, was a massive south and west vista of untouched wilderness backed by ocean.

He wondered how much help she had tending to it. Some man who took care of it, and her?

No.

Not with the way she'd kissed him. He refused to believe that someone who was two-timing him, like his ex-fiancée, could have kissed him like that. Rebecca Monica Monash of the Winnetka Monashs certainly never had.

Devin hurried down the trail. It plunged back into the forest but was far better groomed on this side of the ridge, as if she had nothing left to hide. A wide lane of tamped earth let him move quickly. In a few places, logs had been chainsaw split and buried flat side up as steps. A small bridge crossed an active creek rushing down a narrow gully from somewhere higher up in the Coast Range mountains.

The woods ended abruptly, practically launching him into an open meadow. And there he nearly flattened her.

# # #

Tiffany yelped in shock as a man burst out of the trees. He was filthy, his clothes torn, his face looked as if some woman in her last desperate moments had dragged her nails over his skin, and he held a weapon high in one hand.

Her past had come back!

Somehow it had found her here in what she'd always thought of as her maiden's mountain fastness, safe from the cruel world.

She dropped to the ground, beside the hole she'd been digging, and huddled there in the dirt.

Her final thought was how appropriate it was that she'd dug her own grave.

"Tiffany?"

She kept her head covered, waiting for the blow, the inevitable crashing slap her stepfather had so loved before the true horror began.

"Tiffany?" This time a hand touched her ever so lightly on the shoulder.

When she flinched it jerked away rather than pinning her harder.

"Tiffany, it's…"

Devin.

"…Devin."

She knew the voice. Not her past—no flashback of foul memories. But she couldn't move. Not yet. Though she managed not to flinch when the hand once more brushed her shoulder.

"I'm sorry I scared you."

Which didn't begin to explain what he'd done. Scared and stark terror had no more relation that a smile and ecstasy. It was a black pit from which there was no return. No way back to—

She did her best to shove that aside.

"Devin?" She hadn't meant it as a question, but her throat was too tight to control.

"Yes." And he was helping her to sit up in the dirt.

Her hands remained clenched protectively across her chest, but her feet swung down into the hole. Into the grave.

Into Flo's grave. The little goat had fought bravely through the night and the day to bring her kid into the world. She'd succeeded, but in the end it had cost her own life and it had been beyond Tiffany's skill to save her. It was only the second goat she'd ever lost, and it felt as if a piece of her heart had died along with it.

Her hands were still bloody, her jeans and shirt dark with dried stains of a blood loss she hadn't been able to stop.

"Devin?" This time she managed to turn and face him as he sat on the grave's lip beside her.

"Right here."

He too was a mess. Covered in plaster dust. His face bore a half dozen scrapes that she would now see were minor and not the parallel claw marks left by a panicked woman. One had released a small trickle of blood that had run down his cheek like a tear before it dried.

She'd never seen anything so wonderful in her life and buried her face in his shoulder.

When his arm slipped tentatively around her shoulders, the tears began to flow. And she couldn't stop them. Soon she was weeping for her failure to save Flo and then for her past and then simply because she couldn't stop. Her sides ached with the release, yet Devin simply held her.

He didn't shush her.

He didn't promise it would be alright.

He did nothing but hold her tightly and let her cry. When her tears had turned the plaster dust of his shirt back into muddy plaster, she finally found the ability to rein herself back in before the plaster reset and they became a permanent casting themselves. Her fingers hurt as she unclenched them from their tight fists, and finally patted Devin on the chest in thanks.

That had been her undoing before. After that amazing kiss, she had rested her hand on his chest. It wasn't the strong pecs that had captured her attention, but rather the way he felt. As if her hand had simply belonged on his chest. A warmth. A connection. Like no other she'd ever experienced. And she felt it this time too as she spread her fingers over his shirt.

"Sorry I scared you so badly," he whispered again.

"Not your fault," she managed, and brushed at where she'd been weeping against him. Her efforts did nothing but stir the soggy plaster patch into an even less artistic form than her nose imprint. "Don't take the blame for my past."

And without needing explanation, without asking *what* about her past, he simply hugged her hard against him again, dried blood on her clothes and all.

That's when the laugh started. Small at first, it built inside her until it burst forth, almost as wild and hysterical as the weeping had been. Her sides, already sore, were soon in agony.

Where Devin had unexpectedly accepted her weeping, he pulled back from her laughter.

"What's so goddamn funny?"

"I—" she gasped again, trying to find the air to speak. "I was telling Tall Guy—"

"Tall Guy?"

"My dog. I was telling him…that there was no way…I could make myself…less attractive to my own species."

"Uh-huh."

"That was before I got covered in goat blood," Tiffany brushed at her tears. "God, I'm a mess in so many ways." She found a clean spot on her sleeve and used it to wipe her face and nose clean. "Run, Devin. Take my advice and run while you still have the chance."

"Could do that," he rubbed a hand down her back.

She suddenly really wanted him to stay.

"But I only just got here."

And this time she was able to join in his laugh without lapsing back into man-repelling hysteria.

Then she looked down at their feet, dangling together in the grave, and remembered she had a friend to bury and a newborn kid to nurse.

#

"It seemed too impersonal to use the Bobcat to dig it, but I'm being silly. I'll go get it."

Devin stopped her, picked up the four-foot steel breaker bar, and pounded and levered at the hard soil until the hole was deep enough. She knelt at the edge, scooping out shovelfuls of what he broke free.

Devin was utterly exhausted by the time they finished digging the grave in the hard soil.

The goat looked so small when they put it down in the grave. Once the body was covered, they backfilled it together. Rather than morose words or a dirge, she offered up a song by Little Big Town about all being in the band together. All the while tears trickled quietly down her face. He'd done his best with the harmony line.

"She always liked that song," she managed on a hard swallow.

Then she'd introduced him to Tall Guy on the way back across the property—the biggest damn dog Devin had ever seen. It was hard to tell if he would have survived the encounter if not for Tiffany's chaperonage. The dog clearly felt that Devin was suspect and kept a careful eye on him as he was introduced to the goats.

If the goat in the grave had looked small, the newborn kid looked microscopic. It weighed only three pounds and was the size of a Chihuahua, a small one. When Devin went to lift it, Tall Guy unleashed a deep, earth-rumbling snarl. Tiffany merely patted the beast on the head and collected the tiny newborn herself. They took it back to her yurt with them as the sun was sliding down to the horizon.

The yurt was a revelation. Funky and remote farm had nothing to do with the way Tiffany Mills lived. A large bank of solar cells covered the south slope beside the structure.

The yurt's outer material was a thick, rubberized cloth, and the windows and doors, as real as any he'd install on a normal house, were well finished with wood trim. Once inside, Devin had to stop and stare as Tiffany carried the goat to a small framed-in pen close beside the propane stove. The floor was polished oak, lustrous and rich in grain. A full kitchen and bath had been installed along one wall and sported the finest fittings: a Five Star gas range and oven, a small fridge, and granite counters on cherrywood cabinets. A large oak dining table stood close by the windows and was covered by a puzzle still mostly in a thousand pieces. The bed was covered with an heirloom quality quilt—at least he assumed it was because he'd never seen one look so sharp.

"I still haven't finished the stitching," she indicated a corner that had simple grid rows of wide stitches rather than the elaborate pattern that covered the rest of the quilt.

A large cat lay on the other corner.

"Fitzinger is indeed orca-colored."

"And blobbish," Tiffany agreed as she pet him. "He's angry because it's past dinnertime." She rushed into the kitchen and quickly set a bowl of food on the floor.

Devin had the distinct impression that the cat scowled at him before deigning to go and eat. He wondered just who was the master of the yurt after all.

Devin brushed the cat hair off the quilt and almost blurted out, "You did this?" Tiffany seemed to always make him want to restate the obvious. Instead he managed, "It's already gorgeous."

"Thanks," Tiffany was making up a baby bottle for the goat. "You first."

"Me first what?"

"Shower. Just shake out your clothes, though. I don't think I have anything that would fit you and my only dryer is the wind."

Devin would actually take that as a good sign. No men here. No men leaving clothes behind. *Cad!* But the appellation didn't stick as he soaped and scrubbed. It went right down the drain with the plaster dust and old sweat. Something inside him was more than just charmed by a woman who sang a country rock song over a goat's grave.

The soap stung his face, but soon he was as clean as he was going to get without fresh clothes. He'd spotted the rainwater catchment tanks outside. Unsure if she also had a well, he finished quickly to save water.

Not wanting to beat his mucky clothes clean in her immaculate bathroom, he wrapped a towel around his hips and carried the dirty clothes out onto the deck. He was thankful that Tiffany was too intent on feeding the little goat to notice that her towels weren't exactly thick enough to hide his body's reaction to wandering mostly naked through her home.

By the time he was dressed and ready to go back inside, the light was failing. The entire horizon was dark with thick clouds, but they looked to be far out to sea. The dome of the sky was a deep blue he'd never seen in Chicago. Mesmerized, he watched the last of the color bleed out of the sky.

He decided that this was a good place to be as he could hear the shower start again. Imagining Tiffany so nearby, naked and covered in soap was a dangerous image. Yet she'd invited him here. And while her thinking might be occasionally straightforward, he'd learned over dinner that a very sharp mind lurked behind that reserved, shy facade that she presented to most people. In fact, Greg had stumbled to a halt as he came up behind Tiffany to serve her while she and Devin were talking about how *To Kill a Mockingbird* could be adapted to modern issues. He'd looked down at the back of Tiffany's head wide-eyed, like staring at a lion's (or rather a lioness') lioness) as the cage door at the zoo as it accidently swung open. He had silently delivered her food and rushed away for the safety of his kitchen.

As the meal progressed, Devin had become fascinated by his dinner companion. She was cloistered only in how she lived. Her comments were sharp, perceptive, and deeply observant of the world around her. Though they had stuck mostly to books and movies, her interpretations of thematic congruencies and dissonances (her words) revealed a deeply thoughtful and caring woman.

"Planet light, planet bright," Tiffany whispered as she stepped up beside him on the darkened yurt deck. "First planet I see tonight." He hadn't even heard the shower turn off.

"Where…oh!" Even as he turned his head toward her he spotted the elusive point of light just emerging from the fading brightness of the day. "Which one is it?"

"Venus. Goddess of love and beauty. The Romans also heaped fertility, sex, prosperity, desire, and victory onto her shoulders, which has always struck me as a little bit excessive. If you're going to go with a pantheon rather than a single god, it feels like you're cutting out a lot of potential good jobs for women by giving so many of them to just one. And can you imagine what her in-basket must have looked like back in the day?"

"Ugly," Devin agreed, growing more aware of Tiffany's closeness by the second. It was as if she radiated warmth enough to push back the cooling evening. Perhaps a goddess power of her own.

"No, beautiful. She's the goddess of beauty after all, so of course her in-basket would be beautiful…just crammed very full."

He laughed because of course she was right. He was beginning to have trouble breathing with Tiffany standing so close beside him on the deck.

"Would you—" "I should—"

"You first." "No, you."

When Tiffany didn't continue, Devin finally spoke. "I should get back. It's getting late." Actually it was getting dark and he wondered what evil beasts lurked in the night forest and how he'd find his way through. "What were you going to say?"

"I was going to ask if you'd like some tea or maybe a hot cocoa."

"I'm not so sure that's smart," Devin turned slowly to face her shadowy outline, "because that would mean keeping my hands off you for even longer than I already have."

There was a long silence. Then he heard a fast flutter of wings overhead.

"What the hell?" He ducked when he saw an outline against the sky like no bird he'd ever seen before.

"It's a little brown. I have a colony of those bats living on the north edge of the property; they like the stream there."

"You have a colony of bats? Are they dangerous?"

"Only to bugs."

"Oh." And the silence returned. He should go. He should do the decent thing and start down the steps in front of him. He should—

Then Tiffany stepped into his arms. As fierce as her final hug had been down in the lighthouse meadow, this time it was as soft as her hair. Her kiss wasn't wild or frantic, instead it was lush. A warm, soft, thorough kiss.

"I'm getting you dirty," though he didn't know why he cared. He could smell her clean freshness and knew that he didn't offer the same, not in his construction clothes.

In answer she tugged at the hem of his t-shirt. Before he could protest, she'd yanked it up far enough that he had no choice but to let her take it off the rest of the way.

A shiver slid over his skin, whether due to the night air or in anticipation of holding her just that much closer, he wasn't sure.

"Well, if one of us is going to be half naked," he began unbuttoning the front of her flannel shirt and she didn't stop him. He wished there was enough light to see. He'd imagined what she would look like: strong yet soft, curved but trim from hard work. She always wore loose clothes that, combined with her long hair, kept her form hidden from view. But when he had opened the last button and could slide his hands about her waist, he decided that his imagination was completely lacking in…imagination.

Her skin was so soft and smooth against his palms that he might be holding water. As he pulled her in by sliding his hands up her back, he could feel the muscles ripple beneath her narrow shoulders. And this time when their chests pressed together there was no mere impression of curves. Tiffany wasn't powerfully curved, but neither was she delicately slender—a man who had the good fortune to hold her knew that a woman's breasts pressed against his chest. He levered the shirt off her shoulders and she put her arms back to let it slip away into the darkness.

Unable to resist, he scooped his hands into her hair and then fluttered it outward in a long billow through his fingers. She wrapped her arms around his neck and giggled as he played with it. It was an utterly ridiculous length for someone who lived and worked on a farm and he loved every last inch of it.

He scooped again, this time flipping it up and over both of them so that they were hidden beneath the sliding tresses. This time when he kissed her, beneath the canopy of her hair, the fierce power was back. The fire reached down and grabbed him hard and he pulled her to him as tightly as he could.

# # #

Tiffany could feel the crazy need taking her over again, just like the first time she'd kissed Devin. She considered pulling back—shutting it down, or at least tempering her emotions enough that he wouldn't think she was a lunatic. But he made her feel that way and she had promised herself long ago that feelings were not a game; if she felt them, she'd show them.

Her mother manipulated them like weapons until Tiffany doubted that she would know a true feeling unless it introduced itself with an exceptional stock portfolio. And if her ancestors Lillian and Pearl had managed to speak their true feelings so long ago, perhaps all of their lives would have been different.

And Devin made her feel her emotions—and though they were mostly unfamiliar, they were powerfully wonderful ones. His rough hands on her skin made her so sharply aware of being alive. His strong chest pressed against hers was creating a feedback system of hyperawareness. And his obvious joy while playing with her hair kept making her want to laugh. She'd thought a hundred times about hacking it off. There was no longer any need to hide from aggressors, not in Eagle Cove, especially not in the deep woods on a hidden farm. It was also a reminder of a past when there had been.

But Devin's combing fingers brushed all of those memories away except for Lillian's joy at a man brushing her hair through his hands. Lillian's—

No. Not Lillian's.

Tiffany's joy.

She needed.

That became the overriding sensation. She needed Devin. He made her feel; it had been so long since she'd *felt.* Not just physical sensation but also deep in her chest. It was a crazy mix. Today had held grief, near hysteria, joy, and now…need.

When she started to remove his jeans, he laid a hand over hers.

"I brought no protection."

"I did," she owned precisely one box that she replaced on the expiration date each year, but had never opened. Not once, until she'd come out of the shower to see Devin standing barefoot on her deck, silhouetted against the sunset. Then she knew why she'd kept buying them. This time she wouldn't be throwing them out on their expiration date.

He didn't resist as she finished undoing his pants. As she worked them down his legs, she felt the strength that he had. Devin was neither desk jockey nor weekend warrior; he was a man who used his body and used it hard.

Once he'd stepped out of his pants, she quickly shed her own and then moved back against him. Again that dynamic shock as if their bodies recognized each other beyond all possibility.

Unable to wait, unable to delay her need, she pulled him down onto the deck until he was lying atop her.

"I've never made love out of doors," he whispered to her.

Neither had she. Sex was hidden. Dirty deeds in dark corners. In college and grad school, the few times she had allowed it to occur, it had always been in her own bed. She'd never gone to a boy's room; only in a place that was hers, where she felt safe.

She focused past Devin at the now dark sky and could only gasp in wonder. Behind him, like a perfect tapestry, the stars were slowly filling the sky.

"What?" He froze and asked as if he was afraid he'd hurt her.

"Let's trade places and you'll see."

Instead of some awkward maneuvering, he used his strength to roll them over; a strong hand clamped firmly on her butt to help guide them sent a warmth shooting through her from his hand to her toes.

"I don't—Oh!" His gasp of wonder took her by surprise. She hadn't really expected him to understand the magic of the vast openness. It was just the two of them beneath the whole sweep of the sky. But he did. He understood.

"Now," she managed past a tight throat. She flailed around a hand on the deck until she found her pants pocket and shoved the foil packet into Devin's palm. "Now! Hurry! Please hurry!"

He didn't keep her waiting but a moment. Then with his strong hands guiding her hips, she slid down over him, taking him in. Even first contact had sensations shooting through her. Each rocking of her hips blossomed along her nerves. When he pulled himself up enough to find one of her breasts with his tongue, her body bloomed.

Sex had been enjoyable at times, though she'd never really understood the big deal. But with Devin inside her, coaxing, inviting, welcoming, she flew. Flew until she was lost between the stars and the wonderful man who lay beneath her.

When both of their bodies had at long last ceased shuddering and she lay upon his chest, Tiffany decided that she might never move again.

"Your skin is all goosebumps," Devin whispered as he rubbed his hands over her bottom and held her tight against him.

"You're so romantic," she teased him. Then she blinked at herself in surprise. She'd *teased* him. It was a skill she didn't know she possessed. A skill she'd lacked before this moment.

"How about this?"

He lifted her off him, despite her whimper of protest. With all of the blood surging through her body, how could she ever be cold again?

But then he swept her up into his arms and carried her into the yurt like some movie heroine, which definitely improved his rating on the romantic scale. The small heat lamp over the sleeping kid in its pen filled the interior of the yurt with a soft red glow. Devin carried her to the bed and together they slid under the covers. He then improved his rating even more by not disturbing Fitz, who lay curled up on his pillow. Instead, Devin shared her pillow and pulled her tightly against him until she had no choice but to rest her head on his shoulder, wrap her arm about his wonderful chest, and throw a leg across his hips.

"I guess I was never the most romantic guy, but I can work on that."

She breathed him in until she was almost dizzy with him. "This works great for me just as we are."

"Me too," he sighed, one hand upon her back and the other hooked over her knee. And between one moment and the next, fell asleep.

"How stereotypical," she whispered but couldn't help smiling. There was a man in her bed, something that hadn't happened in a long time. A man that she wanted there more than any other before. He'd said he had to go back to Chicago at some time, but he was here now and she decided that was all that counted.

# # #

Devin woke to a soft bleating sound and wondered where the hell he was. A strange ceiling of upward-sloping 2x4s arranged like slices of a pie.

Another bleat.

Alone in a large bed with—he slid a hand out—a warm spot close beside him. Somewhere in the night Fitz had relinquished the second pillow to Devin.

A whispered, "Hush you. It's almost warm," brought Devin the rest of the way awake. The newborn kid was on its feet in the little pen with its nose pressed hard against the screen; Fitz was curled up just outside the pen but still in the wash of the heat lamp, revealing exactly where his true loyalties lay.

And then an impossible mirage moved across from the shadowed kitchen, holding a baby bottle.

Tiffany, clothed only in her hair, reached into the pen, lifted out the goat, and then sat on the floor with the kid cradled in her lap as it suckled eagerly on the baby bottle. He could only watch in wonder as she fed, soothed, and coddled the tiny creature. Her fair skin was warmed by the small light, or perhaps it was by the love that shone out of her.

The newborn was falling asleep in her lap by the time Tiffany was done, then she gently returned her to the pen. She rose in a fluid motion, her hair floating behind her as she returned the half-empty bottle to the refrigerator.

There was a lithe strength to her movements and a breath-taking beauty to her form. She didn't have the trainer-toned and balanced perfection that Rebecca Monash had achieved. Instead she had a natural reality that could only come from healthy living and hard work.

"Who are you?" Devin asked in wonder as she slid back between the covers.

"Why? Does it matter?" Tiffany's voice was oddly defensive, a tone he hadn't heard from her before.

"No. I mean. Well it does, but that isn't what I was asking."

"Then what were you asking?" She was keeping her distance beneath the covers and he wondered if she could disappear from her own bed as mysteriously as she could when visiting Eagle Cove.

"I barely know you, yet it's like you've hypnotized me. I don't know if I've ever seen something more beautiful than watching you sit there feeding that goat. Your kindness pours out of you. And this farm. Do you really do all this alone?"

"I hired help to set up here, but that was three years ago. You're the first person ever to trespass on my property."

"Trespass?"

He could see her wince. "That didn't come out right."

"Okay," he'd let that go because he supposed he had been trespassing. "I guess what I'm trying to say is, you're one damned impressive woman."

"Really?"

He laughed at the surprise in her voice. "Really. All this and the best sex of my lifetime, for all of it being over way too fast. I—" but he'd keep those other thoughts to himself. He'd wondered if the joy and the need of sex had been burned out of him by Rebecca's betrayal, but Tiffany had just proven that completely wrong.

"Sex." Her voice was flat when she said it.

Devin could have kicked himself. It had been great sex, or certainly the most powerful ever. But "sex" was what you had when it held no meaning. And impossibly, though he'd known her only a week, this had been so much more.

"This was just—"

Unable to stand the flat tone, Devin cut her off with a frustrated growl. "Let me show you what I meant," and he kissed her. She didn't protest, but it was a long and oddly fear-filled moment for him before she gave in and opened to him.

This time it wasn't over too fast, except that he never wanted it to end. The goat had woken them well before dawn. It was well after before he was done showing Tiffany how he felt about her.

Because it was more than just sex. In fact, he was a little unnerved by how much more.

Chapter 5

Tiffany missed Devin even more than she missed Flo, which didn't seem right. Flo had been one of her very first kids, born of Meg. Tiffany had stayed awake for days, sitting in the pen with the goat care books in her lap. She fussed more over the newborn than Meg had, and now Tiffany had buried her.

She could see the other adults looking for their friend, especially Annie who'd been so close to Flo. Her orphaned kid needed such constant care and feeding, that Tiffany slipped her into a sling and carried her through the day. Maybe when Annie finally birthed, she could rub some of the birth matter on the first kid and convince her that she'd delivered two.

But it wasn't to her goats or her garden that her thoughts kept drifting so often.

It was to Devin Robison. The way he'd looked down at her even as the aftermath rippled through her. He might have called it "sex," but she could see in his eyes that it was something more even if he wasn't willing to say it. She wasn't sure that she was either, but had been unable to look away as he searched her face for answers she didn't have.

They'd barely spoken over a breakfast, not out of awkwardness but because there had been no need to chink words into gaps of feeling.

The yurt's air had been thick with feeling and it had been enough to keep them trading smiles as they ate scrambled eggs with a sprinkling of reconstituted dried diced ham that she'd put up last year and early asparagus from her garden. His horror that the eggs had arrived chicken-warm and covered in poo had set her to giggling. Again the hysteria had threatened. She was so out of her element. A beautiful man had twice made love to her, had helped her bury her goat, and had left her with such a sweet kiss before heading back down the trail.

How was she *not* supposed to think about him and that confident male stride as he'd headed off across her land? In the distance she'd seen him stop at the very edge of her property. He spent a few minutes there, then she heard the soft banging sound on the breeze as he drove a branch into the ground to mark Flo's grave, using his abandoned crowbar as a hammer.

Or not think about his invitation to go sailing tomorrow morning. The only time she left the farm other than for knitting had been the weddings of Jessica, Becky, and now Natalya and Gina. Going to town on a Sunday felt wild, even a little dangerous, but perhaps in a good way.

That was the most intrusive thought that Devin had left behind. Had she spent too much time alone up on her mountain? Too used to only her own company?

The odd thing was that in Eagle Cove she was a far more social person than she'd ever been in her life. For three years, the women of Eagle Cove had welcomed her, let her sit with them, be with them, all without making any demands upon her.

Devin had intruded on her property, her thoughts, and was now starting to slip his way into her heart. Her heart was hers, it belonged to no one. That was a lesson hard learned.

But Jessica was happy with her Greg, despite her whining complaints about her pregnancy. And Becky's and Natalya's happiness was unmistakable as well. They didn't just stand by their men, they gave their hearts to them.

"I don't know if I can ever do that," she told Tall Guy.

He rolled his eyes at her without even bothering to raise his head off his forepaws.

"Come on, you." She let him out of the goat pen and led him off into the woods to help check the rabbit snares.

"Maybe I'll just skip tomorrow's sailing." Though she'd never been out on a boat despite growing up in San Francisco. It would be a new experience. As if Devin Robison wasn't enough new experience.

And there he was again, back in the center of her thoughts, making her body tingle at just the memory of his touch.

"Or maybe I will go."

Tall Guy didn't look at all surprised as she changed her mind for the hundredth time this morning.

He still didn't look surprised when she petted him the next morning before heading down the trail with little Shprintze riding in a sling under her arm.

\# \# \#

Devin had been at the trailhead by seven-thirty because he was pitiful. He'd said eight-thirty, but he'd thought that it would be more decent if he hiked up and called for her at her door.

But would that be trespassing? She'd said it that way, *You're the first person to ever* trespass *on my property*. Maybe he shouldn't go without an invitation.

Which had left him cooling his heels in the lighthouse meadow for half an hour and wondering if instead he might have offended her for not returning after work the previous night and now she wouldn't come. Again he stood at the trailhead.

No, he decided again. Too pushy.

Then he wondered if he'd been too high pressure by even inviting her out. It sounded suspiciously like a date. To kill time, he couldn't go to work on the cottage; it would just make him all dirty again. Instead he pulled out the half-finished plans and unrolled them on the hood of the truck.

It took him forever to shift his thoughts from the full-body sendoff he'd received yesterday morning to the cottage's redesign, but he finally managed.

He'd add a porch, one big enough to sit under on a warm day and stay dry under while unlocking the door on a wet one. But it also had to be small enough and the right form to fit in without breaking the cottage's exterior charm.

The inside…was still puzzling him. He couldn't yet see what direction he wanted to take the décor yet. The room layout was easy. Because it would be changing from a lighthouse keeper's family into private rooms, he'd have to add several baths. Gina had cleared the idea to make a larger suite out of two of the upstairs rooms, which had saved him finding somewhere for a second staircase. There would be a small kitchenette on the ground floor, but breakfast would still be down at the big Victorian, which simplified that. It would allow him to convert the old dining and kitchen area into an additional cozy room which offset the doubled room upstairs.

A week to finish the teardown and muck out. Two weeks upgrading wiring and plumbing. Another to inspect, insulate, sheetrock. That would leave two months to refloor and do all of the detailed finish and trim work. If everything went according to plan, he could be back in Chicago by September for the tail end of the building season.

Maybe if he…

And there she was. One of her inevitable flowy shirts, this one a russet orange, a light jacket carried loosely in one hand and a tiny goat head peering at him from a sling under her other arm.

"Are you planning to say hello?"

Tiffany was so damned beautiful, the sun shining upon her hair as if she had indeed been manifested anew right at this moment. Star Trek transportered into place. Unable to speak, he circled the truck.

"Your plans!"

He heard them curl back up, roll off the truck's hood, and plop into the dirt. To hell with his plans.

Careful of the tiny goat, but nothing else, he scooped Tiffany against him and kissed her hard. She tasted like heaven. Her soft sigh of pleasure had him considering how she'd feel lying naked beneath him on his truck bed, if he cleared all of the scrap lath out of it.

Something hard fisted him in the ribs. Hard enough to make him break the kiss though Tiffany had tipped her head back and wrapped her arms about his neck.

The baby goat butted him again.

"Hey!" He blocked the third blow with the palm of his hand.

"I don't think that Shprintze likes you much," Tiffany had loosened her arms enough to look down between them without letting go.

"Tevye's fourth daughter?"

"How did you know that?"

"I played Perchik in a high school production back in Chicago." Back in happier, simpler times.

"Do you like acting?"

"No, but Hodel was awfully hot." Then he felt stupid for saying it.

"And did Perchik get his Hodel?" Her smile was forgiving of his own clumsiness.

"He did," he admitted and couldn't stop the smile. They'd ended up going to the junior prom together, a night that had cost them both their virginity. An event they'd commemorated thoroughly and much less awkwardly at their senior prom. "She's now a high-end entertainment attorney in Los Angeles married to one of her superstar clients."

"Is she the one who got away?"

"What? Her? No! I— We— The one—" He sighed. "Crap! No. It wasn't like that. It was a high school thing. Awesome but nothing permanent. How about you? Tell me about the one who slipped away."

And he felt her freeze. Felt her, for just an instant, become as frozen as she'd been when she'd gone fetal on the ground beside her goat's grave.

He did the only thing he knew how to do: he held her tight—as tightly as he could while keeping a protective palm against the kid's forehead.

"Okay. Bad question. Just ignore it. Okay? Just pretend I'm asking about Shprintze. Please?"

She nodded against his shoulder, her face planted in the same spot it had been yesterday. He hoped she didn't start crying again—he didn't know if he could stand to hear the heartrending pain of it again.

"Just know," he told the top of her head. "If I ever meet the bastard who did whatever he did to you, I'm going to kill him. No questions asked."

Tiffany pulled back enough to look at him. Her eyes were swimming, but they weren't spilling over.

Devin met her gaze as it shifted from pain to assessment.

"You would, wouldn't you?"

"In a heartbeat." He'd never so much as punched a man before. But he also didn't doubt that if confronted with the bastard who had so hurt this beautiful woman, he wouldn't hesitate.

"Then you'll be glad…no, wrong word. You'll…want to know that you'll never have to worry about that. Someone else already got to him." She met his gaze levelly despite whatever horror-memory he'd just dug up twice in two days.

"Damn," he barely managed a whisper.

"Sorry you missed your chance?"

"No. Busy wondering what it is about Eagle Cove that makes their women so spectacularly strong."

Her smile went radiant.

But he forgot one thing as he leaned back in to renew their kiss.

The next moment he was on his knees in the dirt. Shprintze the goat had head-butted him squarely in the solar plexus.

# # #

Tiffany didn't need to be familiar with the docks on Eagle Bay to know which boat belonged to Hector Jackson because there weren't that many to choose from. The McCall and Baxter fishing boats both had large charter signs on them. And both were busy loading up with whale watch charters as the big grays were busy migrating north along the Pacific Coast.

There were also a half dozen small fishing skiffs and one big sailboat.

She wished she hadn't said anything to Devin about her past, but she had. To make matters worse, she hadn't been able to think of a thing to say on the drive to the marina and had left Devin to fill in the silences. It didn't take him long to understand. Then he quieted and simply reached out to take her hand in his. He held it as he drove one-handed into and through town.

She'd read the literature. Some men were repulsed by knowing a woman had been molested. Other, creepier ones, were attracted by the idea. Not wishing to experience either reaction, she had never told anyone a single word of her past after escaping high school. She'd been re-born at eighteen…until today.

Devin's reaction, she should have known in advance but she hadn't, was completely different. He simply took her hand and held it as if nothing had happened. No, that wasn't right either. He did it as if…it didn't matter. That was quite different. It made all the difference in the world and she held on tighter as he drove.

He's going to leave eventually, she reminded herself. But the inner Tiffany didn't care. She'd seen the truth of his fury and was touched by the simple tenderness with which he held her hand. It was enough.

The sailboat was huge. Devin had said it was a Pearson 42 and she'd spent quite a bit of time online looking up sailboats last night. At first she'd wanted to see what she'd foolishly agreed to, but had soon become fascinated. She had a satellite connection for her Internet and a sat-phone for emergencies…a device she never used except for her twice yearly check-ins that her attorney in California had insisted on. "Want to know you're alive, Ms. Mills. Hear your voice, make sure you're okay." The calls were consistently brief and relatively painless. In retrospect, even appreciated.

Her study had started with the Pearson 42, but she hadn't been able to understand a word of it. That led her into basic sailboat diagrams with all the parts labeled, which had led her into a vast glossary of nautical terms she'd only been able to partly absorb. She'd eventually backtracked to the Pearson 42 and was able to make some sense of it. First of all, 42 meant forty-two feet long.

She also knew that it was often in the top-ten lists for cruising sailboats as distinct from racers and daysailers—the three primary classifications of sailboats. Cruiser meant comfort over long distances and the boat appeared as if it had done a lot of travel. It was neat and appeared to be in good repair, but it looked very…lived in.

At the boat, Hector waved a cheerful greeting.

"Have you sailed before, Tiffany? No? Well, your young man thinks he has. What say we prove him wrong?"

Tiffany stood uncertainly on the dock. Nothing in her research had said how to board a sailboat. The deck rose three feet above the dock, white with a hand-wide red line by the water and a blue one just below the—she couldn't remember the word, perhaps she hadn't found one—the place where deck met hull, built as separate pieces then bonded together. She didn't see a place to crawl between the wires, there was netting attached to the inside of the long safety lines.

Nor had any of her history told her how to respond to Hector's "your young man." She eyed the length of the dock leading toward town, but Devin still held her hand—which she supposed made the "your young man" assumption more valid than she was prepared for.

Using it, Devin led her back—aft—to a short set of stairs at an opening through the boat's lifelines. He helped her up and then stepped up beside her. She almost lost her balance at the unexpected shift in the deck when he boarded. There were some things she couldn't learn online.

"You can put your coats down below, Devin. It's a warm morning, though it may be cooler out on the water."

Devin took hers and headed below. Tiffany set the sling gently down on the knee-high doghouse—no, that was for oversized cabins—cabin roof.

"Is that a goat?" Hector inspected the bundle.

Tiffany opened the sling further for Hector to look inside. "She's newborn and lost her mother. I couldn't leave Shprintze for a whole day. I hope that's okay."

"I don't think that's up to me."

"But it is your boat?"

"No, ma'am. Belongs to the ship's master. Lieutenant Commander Queeg by name, LC Queeg for medium, Q for short."

"Queeg as in *The Caine Mutiny?* The mad commander played by Humphrey Bogart?"

"The same."

At that moment a big, gray-and-black striped cat trotted up on deck using the same door—gangway? companionway? hatch!—that Devin had used to go below. The cat hopped up onto the cabin roof and trotted over to Tiffany.

Hector stood stiffly and snapped a sharp salute that the cat ignored as any egotistical senior officer might. After a sniff and a scratch accepted from Tiffany with a very feline hauteur, LC Queeg inspected the sleeping kid.

Tiffany stood poised to make a grab if the cat didn't approve. LC Queeg was at least twice the size and four times the weight of Shprintze.

After a moment, the cat turned to look up at Hector.

"You tell me, Commander."

The cat then crawled onto the blanket and curled up around the goat. Shprintze woke enough to lift her head and rest it over the cat's belly before going back to sleep. Q began cleaning the baby goat.

"Be damned," Hector said softly. "He's never been a big fan of four-footed strangers on his boat. Nor winged ones. He's been known to face down angry seagulls twice his size if they board without proper orders. Well, let's leave them be." A handrail stuck up along the cabin's roof ensured that they stayed in place, not that the fall from cabin to deck was high enough to cause more than surprise.

He led her forward and she began learning about what had only been pictures and labels last night.

Devin hadn't returned from inside the boat—below. She wondered what he was learning down there.

# # #

Devin had meant to drop their jackets on the first level surface and head back up the companionway ladder, but he was stopped by the beauty of the boat's interior. The ones he'd been in before were just daysailers: a fiberglass bunk covered in sailbags and old life vests, a cooler jammed into a corner and filled with beer, maybe a radio.

This was exquisite. There were teak decking and trim, brass fittings, and absolutely no straight lines. Everything was a curve, the joinery work was a thing of beauty. The wood was bright with multiple coats of varnish and smooth as no sander could achieve—it required decades of constant use and patient upkeep to make wood look like this.

He poked though the galley: top-loading fridge, a counter that lifted to reveal a three-burner propane stove, a small but utilitarian two-basin sink. Quaint and impressively efficient.

Doing this in the cottage could save half the kitchenette space or more.

Tiffany's and Hector's footsteps, moving about the deck over his head, let him follow their progress. But he continued his inspection—right until it almost ran him head-on into Dragon Winslow. She'd been sitting quietly at a teak table that could seat three—no, it had a drop-leaf, it could seat six, three on either side of the table.

"You *are* a carpenter then," her greeting was abrupt, but no longer struck fear into his heart.

"This is beautiful work," he sat on a bench seat across from her, long enough that it could double as a narrow bunk, and rubbed a hand over the worn trimwork around a tiny propane heater. The heater would probably be enough to keep the whole boat warm on a cold night. The stove itself was burnished steel. "Beautiful."

"I felt that this might provide you with proper perspective for the lightkeeper's cottage."

"It does. It really does." Then he looked at her instead of the beautiful boat. "Thank you."

"Well," she sniffed, "you have some manners."

"I try not to let them get in my way." That earned him her first real smile since he'd met her.

"I hear," she nodded up toward the steps moving back and forth on the deck, "that you managed to coax Tiffany from her lair."

And he remembered their first meeting, when Dragon Winslow had asked questions that Tiffany had done her best to avoid. Then he began to wonder if he was not the purpose of today's invitation, but rather Tiffany was the target. Had the Dragon used him and Hector to isolate Tiffany on the boat where she couldn't avoid questioning? He remembered her hunching response at every question into her past, never mind the full-blown panic he'd caused when he surprised her.

He rose back to his feet. "I brought her as my guest. To sail. No more. I will not have that trust violated. Shall I take her and go?" He'd never spoken this way to anyone. He ran his crews by cheering them along, teaching them quietly what they didn't know. Of all people to take on, he'd chosen the Dragon. He braced for her talons.

She regarded him for a long time.

He held her gaze even as the boat rocked back and forth beneath the motions of Hector and Tiffany above. He could hear her asking questions and Hector instructing. Soon it would be awkward to leave, very soon. Better to face it. With their jackets still clenched in his hand, he turned for the ladder.

Then the Dragon laughed. But it was not mean or dangerous as it should be from a dragon. Rather it was amused.

"Well, that will teach me, and with a dose of my own medicine," she shook her head. "You have honor, Devin Robison. And you protect what you care about."

"I do," which was something of a surprise at the moment. Just how much he cared about Tiffany Mills.

"I shall offer you a bargain."

"I'm listening," but Devin didn't turn to fully face her. *I'm still ready to go* he was saying.

"I shall reserve my interest in what she is hiding…"

"If I do what?"

"Bright boy," she rose to stand in front of him. "If you let me know when she is ready to speak with me."

"And if she never is?"

"Then I shall suffer in silence. At least for as long as I can manage. So do not make me wait too long."

"Some bargain."

"It is the best I can offer. That girl has always been a puzzle. I care for her a great deal, which is actually why I will push if I must. I suspect that the puzzle piece she hides may be close to the heart of what troubles her." Then she left him and climbed back up onto the deck.

No, he knew what troubled her, and could feel his hands clench into fists at even the thought. That would not be why she wasn't talking to the Dragon. There was more than that going on…and not just about herself.

Care for her a great deal. Devin sat back down and stared at the fine woodwork, but he couldn't focus on it.

Care for her a great deal? He did.

Devin scrubbed at his face. He was in so far over his head.

# # #

Tiffany had always avoided invitations to go sailing before. The reason was easy to recall now, though she hadn't thought of it when Devin had invited her.

April 1900

I am so sore of heart as I stand ashore and observe the departure of his ship. My very soul aches that Ernest must leave Eagle Cove, yet he is a foremast hand with a four-year contract.

Our time together was so brief, but I shall be ever thankful that he was led to me. By his word, I shall look for his return in the summer, when I may once more feel the ecstasy that he can evoke from my willing body. In summer then, I may once more wrap my arms and legs about him and again call him "mine."

Tiffany had never wanted to intrude upon the memory of Lillian's departing lover. By always choosing to remain ashore, Tiffany could relive Lillian's moment when Ernest had still been true and the future filled with hope.

But over a century had passed and Tiffany had willing consented to accompany Devin before she could think to refuse. And was gloriously happy that she had. She tried to remember when she had so enjoyed herself. There was something about being out on a sailboat. She could leave the land behind and some part of her natural timidity with it.

For just this once, this lone sunny morning sliding over the water under the pressure of a steady breeze, she could pretend she was someone else. No, she didn't want to be someone else. Didn't want to hide in her ancestor's memories. Perhaps she could pretend that she was her better self…and Devin made that the simplest of all choices. Tiffany lay back against his chest in the cockpit. He had one arm about her waist and they each had a hand on the wheel. This was *her* moment of heaven.

Once the animals were safely out of the way, Hector had given them lessons back and forth across the bay. Finally he'd announced that Tiffany was ready and there was, with a broad wink, at least some hope for Devin. Then he'd headed them out the mouth of the Eagle River and onto the ocean. The forty-two-foot boat made easy work of the six-foot rollers. They were soon sliding south, well off the shore.

She watched the land as they left it behind, curious to see if she could somehow spot herself as they passed. Town gave way to houses. A couple ran along the beach; by his massive stature and her dark hair, she would guess it was Cal Jr. and Natalya freshly returned from their honeymoon. The small dog chasing along at their heels confirmed the identification of the tiny figures.

Soon she saw the two grand Victorians, the one owned by the Slaters that had been Lillian's and the one that had never left the Lamont family. What had been Ernest's thoughts as he sailed this route aboard his lumber schooner? Affection? Love? A belief, at least in that moment, that he would return? Perhaps other, darker thoughts that Tiffany did not want to consider on this beautiful day.

"Look," she pointed out for Devin after they'd passed south of the Orca Head lighthouse. "It appears so small from here."

"Your farm," Devin had followed her direction. "It might look small, but that makes it no less important."

And when he said it, she knew it was true. From out on the water it looked like little more than a cleared patch in the forest. A brilliant reflection of the sun off a solar panel lasted only a moment. But there was her home. There she and Devin had made love. It was enough.

She returned to the sailboat in her thoughts and let Lillian, Ernest, and her farm continue without her for now.

The sounds here seemed so natural. A gull's cry overhead, the shushing of the water along the hull, and the wind as it drove them on. Even the occasional ping of a line against the aluminum mast or the ripple-slap of the three sails felt completely natural. Two "headsails" (pronounced heads'ls by those in the know, which she now was) rose before the mast, which made this boat a cutter-rigged sloop. The big main stretched along the boom from the mast to well past the cockpit.

She tugged lightly down on the marlinspiked wheel to correct for a wave pushing them off their course.

"Marlinspike—the art of rope weaving and knotwork, often decorative, employed by sailors to pass time on long passages." Hector had confirmed, "Technically that's the name of the tool used, but it is often used to describe the fancier knotwork as well. When everything is going right, which isn't often, a single man has a lot of time when crossing one of the ponds. That's what sailors call the seven seas."

"The Ionian, the Aegean, the Black—"

Hector had laughed. "Okay, little lady. So, you know your history. Ponds are the big oceans. The modern seven seas."

It had been fun to tease him, and that thought had been surprising enough for her to lapse into silence until lunchtime came around. Hector and Mrs. Winslow went below to fix sandwiches, leaving just herself and Devin alone on deck. The cat had gone below in search of treats and the kid had drunk a half-bottle of formula and was asleep again on a blanket in the natural cage of the cockpit's raised sides and benches.

"Devin?"

"Mmm?" he murmured into her hair.

"Can we just stay out here?"

"Sure."

"Forever?"

"Works for me," he agreed lazily, tightening his arm about her waist.

Tiffany hadn't quite meant it the way it sounded in her head. Princess Tiffany seeking a happily ever after. But it was the first time she'd ever been so comfortable around other people. Usually she only achieved this when she was alone. And that meant the farm and there was always something begging to be done there. It was quiet and calm, but in a curious way the State of Tiffany wasn't as peaceful as sailing.

"I'll buy you a boat," Devin continued on the prior topic which she had somehow circled around to in her thoughts. "A beautiful one like this that we'll moor in Eagle Bay. Whenever the wind is up, we'll scoot out onto the sea. I could even host tourist evenings on the sea."

"Perish the thought," Hector said from where he'd stuck his head and shoulders through the hatchway to hand plates and sodas out into the cockpit.

"Why?" Tiffany wouldn't do it because she wouldn't want to speak to all of those people, but Hector had seemed a very gregarious and easygoing man. A good counterpoint to the staunch propriety of the woman that Tiffany couldn't address as any other than Mrs. Winslow.

"Tourists are a cruel thing to do to a perfectly nice boat. I've chartered a bit over the years, passing the time in one port or another."

"But once you've sailed with them, don't they become friends?"

Hector handed her a roast beef sandwich on rye and set the next one on the opposite bench for Mrs. Winslow.

"Well, seems they do sometimes." And Hector's smile said that sometimes they became more than that. Then he glanced below without quite looking. Apparently he was hoping to become more than friends with someone else after taking her sailing.

Tiffany couldn't quite school her expression fast enough and Hector saw that he'd been caught. He offered a sheepish smile and a shrug.

"You don't have to worry about me," Tiffany whispered just loud enough for him to hear. "But I'd be careful around Jessica and Natalya."

"Careful about what?" Devin asked as he took the next pair of sandwiches, having missed everything else that was going on.

"Careful of your heading, Mr. Robison," Hector answered curtly and handed across some cans of soda. Then he ducked back below.

"Careful about what?" Devin asked her.

He really was very cute. Handsome, but cute as well.

"You mean about Hector wanting to date Mrs. Winslow?"

Though not as blind as she'd thought a moment before.

"About *what?*" The Dragon snapped from halfway out the companionway hatch.

Devin winced. "She didn't know yet?" Devin whispered to Tiffany.

She shook her head ever so slightly.

"Oops!" He mouthed to her.

Still cute.

It was well past lunch before the Dragon spoke to Hector again and the poor man had no idea why.

# # #

It was midafternoon before they headed back into Eagle Bay. Devin had decided that being in over his head was a good thing, at least when it came to being attracted to Tiffany. They had drifted lazily together all day, whether fighting the wind and bucking the tide or sliding quietly along wing-and-wing, with the sails spread wide to either side to catch the soft tailwind.

Tiffany had unabashedly leaned against him, held hands, and teased him below with a searing kiss that had fired up both his body and his need for her.

Now they sat on the bow to offer Hector and Mrs. Winslow some privacy. He had followed Tiffany forward as she had followed the goat. She had Shprintze on a thin lead attached to a harness Hector had fashioned. The other end was tied about her wrist, just in case the goat found a way overboard. Hector had no animal-sized life preservers aboard as Commander Q had utterly refused to wear them—a tale Hector had told well this afternoon while the Commander slept in his lap.

Devin contemplated the approaching land. They were far enough out that it was still in miniature—a raised hand could block it from sight, from Greg and the Judge's diner to the Lamont B&B where he had first met and played music with Tiffany. Only the lighthouse and the knowledge of Tiffany's farm over the brow of the hill remained visible, until a shift of the boat blocked those as well.

Today was Sunday.

"A week ago this was a foreign stretch unlike anything I'd ever seen before."

"And now?" Tiffany leaned back against the sloped front of the cabin. The goat had once again wound her lead around a couple of deck fixtures and one of his ankles before curling up in Tiffany's lap.

He leaned back beside her. "It's still a mystery, just for different reasons."

"Tell me."

"There's real community here. It's almost as if the more you try to resist it, the stronger it pulls you in."

Tiffany nodded. "You have no idea."

"I know that there's a circle of women who would gladly castrate me if I were to harm a single lovely hair on your head. And I don't think that's an exaggeration."

"You mean like actually…" she made a snipping motion with her forefingers.

"Natalya promised it in as many words. While I was sitting with you at knitting the other day, Jessica held aloft her knitting scissors to make it clear that she'd do it herself if I wasn't careful."

"And others are ready to make our bridal bower."

"Becky," Devin sighed. If he didn't propose soon, Becky might do it for him. "It's been an interesting week."

At that moment his phone rang. They must be close enough to land to get a signal. He pulled it out and answered without thinking.

"D.R. Builders. Devin here."

"Hi, Dev honey."

Devin almost choked, "Rebecca."

"Hi, honey. It's been a while. I was just chatting with Mama and thinking about you." Her tone was honeyed. He could picture her sitting on the back terrace, a fresh gin and tonic on the table, looking down across the expansive front lawn to Lake Michigan. Sure enough he could hear the wind in the phone's microphone. Her blond hair would be down, swishing gently in the breeze. And her mother sitting close by her side, monitoring every word.

"What do you want?"

"Is that any way to talk to your fiancée? No, sorry. I don't want to fight."

That was a good thing. Her method of fighting was shrill or tear-laden or with her claws out (though always careful not to chip a nail). He'd never been much good at fights and tended to fold to avoid them no matter what form they took.

"I miss you, Dev. I know that you had to have your little pout, but I'm sure you're ready to come back now. We need to pick a date." He could actually hear Rebecca's mother in the background, coaching her softly to say the last line. No surprise there; they thought exactly alike.

Devin pulled the phone away to stare at it for a moment. The screen reported, "Rebecca Monica Monash." She'd insisted that he program her full name into his phone when she'd spotted that it only said, "Rebecca."

This was real, not some nightmare.

Tiffany was trying to get up, but she was all snarled in the goat's lead, and was trying to figure out how to extricate herself without waking Shprintze.

Devin, in turn, attempted to rise, but the goat had somehow wrapped her lead string around both of his ankles. He motioned to Tiffany that it was okay to stay and she subsided back to the deck.

He put the phone back to his ear, "You're kidding, right?"

"Oh Dev. You know Mikal was just payback for that little spat we'd had."

He didn't recall "a little spat." Actually there'd been any number of them, but he had no idea which one she was referring to. Rebecca's relationship tactics included always being on the offensive; something he hadn't understood until this moment. Maybe he could play this game too, for once.

"Mikal moved on, didn't he?"

"No man ever leaves me," her denial was emphatic. Yet he knew Mikal had.

"And you discovered that Dad isn't letting him have any piece of the business."

Her brief silence confirmed that.

Dad might have no morals about what women he bedded, but he protected CMC like the shrewd CEO he was. He and Devin had had frank discussions of Mikal's inabilities in business of any type. He could lose money sitting alone in a quiet room.

"It's not that, Dev. I miss you. I want you back."

"Not going to happen."

"But Dev-vin," she always said it that way when she was frustrated enough to use his full name. "You know what I can do for you."

And he'd expected her to start listing some vacation or—

"Magnuson," she named one of the biggest real estate speculators in Chicago, "has always been sweet on me. You know I could get an exclusive contract for CMC. And that's not all. There are others."

Sure. Others she or her mother had slept with. If they couldn't deliver the contracts with offers of sex, or perhaps more sex, they'd probably blackmail the men by threatening to reveal themselves to the men's families.

"Goodbye, Rebecca."

"Oh come on, Devy. You know that you'll never have a woman half as good as me. I can do things for you. Or…I can do things to you. Is that what you want? A little S&M? I've got this black-leather lingerie and cuffs in my bottom dresser drawer. You can use my riding crop and we could—"

Devin yanked the phone away from his ear. He didn't want to hear it. He could hear that she was still going on. He couldn't even stand to touch the disconnect button below her name.

At a loss for what else to do, he heaved the phone as high and hard as he could. It arced up into the sky, tumbled in the wind, flashing as it reflected sunlight, then disappeared into the face of a rolling wave without a sound.

Devin could only stare straight ahead and wonder at the narrowness of his escape. He had almost married *that*.

"From the half I could hear," Tiffany said softly, "I'm guessing that didn't go well."

He turned from looking ahead to looking at her. "My wedding was six weeks ago today."

Tiffany flinched.

Devin caught at her arm to keep her in place. "I didn't go through with it."

"You were almost married and then—what? Go bounce the poor girl who lives alone in the woods?" Fury. He'd never expected Tiffany to be capable of fury.

"No. I— Just hang on and—" Then he groaned and told her the whole sordid story. Not about who his family was, but about the wedding, his brother, the social media, and their reactions, all telling him he was wrong. Right down to his father offering to share his secretary with him. He had to look away while telling the story to hide his own shame.

Tiffany calmed and listened and, by the end of it, was even looking sympathetic, once it was clear that she wasn't just some rebound girl.

"I couldn't stand it anymore. And then that," he waved toward where he'd thrown his phone overboard. "She offered to— Let's just say that your goats have more morals than anyone in Chicago."

"Even when they're rutting?" Tiffany teased him.

"Especially then. Rebecca just offered to deliver me anybody needing a building contractor by sleeping with him."

"You were right. Maybe they should meet my mother."

"Part of the reason she's so mad is you'll never guess who my brother bedded next."

"Your father's secretary?"

"Nope, turns out he'd already been there and done that. Rebecca's married sister was next—the two can't stand each other, rivals since they were toddlers. When Rebecca caught them together in the sauna, Mikal started comparing their sexual performances in some detail. 'So that they could learn from each other's shortcomings how to better please a man.' He, of course, had to tell me all about it, smug bastard."

"Eww!"

"I couldn't agree more. That was when I took the job rebuilding the lightkeeper's cottage." Devin slumped low enough to rest his head back against the cabin and stare up at the sky. "And now a week later I've met dozens of people, people who I wouldn't introduce to my family for fear of alienating them."

"Of alienating your family?"

"No. Of scaring off the wonderful people I've met here." Then he turned and looked at her for the first time since he'd started the story. "I especially don't want them scaring you off."

"Ha!" Tiffany practically laughed in his face. "You can't scare me with family. Someday I'll have to tell you about mine. Starting with my stepfather who—"

He could see the shift in her face. "Don't!"

"Don't what?" Tiffany blinked at him caught halfway to inner fury.

"Don't tell me about it."

"Why not?"

"That's past. I don't want you to *have* to remember a single thing from your past. But mostly because I don't want you to feel utterly sullied the way I do right now."

# # #

"That did it," Tiffany whispered.

"Did what?" Devin looked at her, puzzled.

In answer she pulled him to her, pulled him down to kiss her. She could feel how stiff and angry he was, but slowly, ever so slowly, he shifted out of his past and into their present.

Their kiss was different this time. It wasn't about heat, need, passion, or just feeling so incredibly good. It went deeper. It was about meaning, joy, and connection. Had Lillian and Ernest felt this, or had they only had heat and need? If so, for the first time Tiffany pitied her ancestor rather than envying her.

Devin slipped his arms about her, careful not to disturb the sleeping kid still warm in her lap. Devin saw her as a beautiful woman—who wasn't a basket case-recluse-unholy mess—and for him, it became true.

She felt like all of the things he'd called her: beautiful, strong, powerful. Born anew. A woman with no past except what she chose. For Tiffany now understood that she had the power to choose.

When the kiss finally ended by some mutual agreement, he still held her close, tucked under his arm and facing the wind and the future together.

Yes, that absolutely did it.

Tiffany hadn't understood. Not by watching Jessica, Becky, or Natalya fall in love and marry. Nothing that had happened for Peggy or Gina had taught her what to expect. Not even reading Lillian's diary.

Tiffany breathed in deeply as she faced whatever was to come. She no longer felt any fear, because now she knew what love felt like. Really knew.

And whether Devin stayed for just the summer or for a lifetime, he had changed her for the better. Forever.

Chapter 6

*O*kay, *perhaps not forever.*

Tiffany sat in the brewery with the rest of the knitters on Tuesday and still couldn't seem to find her voice. There was merry chatter going on about the circle as always, but silence had wrapped around her so tightly over the years that she had as little to say as ever.

Yet when Devin had come to her, walking her home last Sunday night and again returning with the evening light on Monday, she hadn't been able to stop talking.

They spoke of growing up in different parts of the country, of people they'd met, of goats and dogs and farming. It was as if all the silence that had stoppered her for a lifetime now spilled forth. They made love then would talk for hours, after all, they had to keep their priorities straight and she could never tire of Devin's strong hands and gentle touch.

Sleep? She'd never slept so little since she used to cower in the dark, waiting in terror. And she'd never felt so awake. In Devin's presence she had become the manic version of herself and had kept apologizing, but couldn't seem to stop, even after the times that he laughed more at her than with her. She would try to be angry about that, but he laughed at his own shortcomings just as easily, and his laugh inevitably called forth her own.

There were things Devin wasn't saying. Which was only fair; there were things she wasn't either. Deciding she was in love with him didn't mean that she'd gone stupid or incautious. It just meant that she was wallowing in the joy of it the way a newborn goat wallowed in discovery of tall meadow grass bathed in warm sunlight.

But as much as she was transformed in his presence, she was still very much herself around others. Mrs. Winslow couldn't have missed that kiss, the boat wasn't all that big. But then neither had Tiffany missed the rather more than neighborly kiss that Mrs. Winslow left with Hector in thanks for the day's sailing trip.

At Tuesday knitting, she and Mrs. Winslow didn't exchange so much as a word, though they did end up sitting side by side on one of the couches. Dragon Winslow was just as gruff, taciturn, and roughly affectionate to everyone as was her norm.

And Tiffany was as silent as ever, despite the transformation Devin had wrought inside her.

"I can't even see my knitting. My belly pushes it too far away," Jessica was complaining. She was propped in a big armchair, cushioned by pillows and with an empty beer keg pushed close beside her seat. Becky had placed a scrap of plywood on top of it as an impromptu table that was kept stocked with tea, finger sandwiches that May Conklin had made up at the Plover Inn, and cookies that Natalya had swiped from the bakery.

"Can't wait," Becky chimed in.

"Are you…?" Half a dozen of the women spoke at once.

"Not yet," Becky's sigh was splendidly dramatic.

Why couldn't Tiffany be more like that?

"We're not even trying, though we're certainly practicing often enough," she offered one of her cheery laughs that spread among the women. "I promised Harry that he'd get a year of peace and quiet for his first year as a judge. Seven months and counting."

"But you've only been married for three months so far," Natalya pointed out. "Come on, Becky. Basic math. Ten months is not a year."

"What he doesn't know won't hurt him," Becky giggled happily. "I don't know if I can stand to wait even that long. Besides, who says it happens the first time you try?"

"Me," Jessica groaned from her chair. "I thought it might take months, or years. Nope."

"Lucky!" Becky declared. "You were always the lucky one. You got married first."

"And pregnant first," Natalya put in.

"And you had a fine writing career," Mrs. Winslow said approvingly.

"You only say that because she followed in your reporter footsteps," Gina teased her.

"She always was a smart girl," Mrs. Winslow countered. Which nobody could argue with because she'd been class valedictorian and was now excelling as Eagle Cove's marketing manager.

"If I'm so damned smart, how come I can barely count stitches anymore? Every time I get to eight, I think of how long I've been pregnant. Fourteen since Greg first kissed me."

"Now she's just bragging," Natalya reached out a hand to brush it over her friend's hair.

"Show off!" Becky agreed.

"Feed her some orange juice," Tiffany suggested quietly.

Mrs. Winslow actually snorted with laughter and several others joined in.

"Gods no!" Jessica held up her hands in terror. "I can't get within a dozen feet of the stuff without this one breaking into a conga dance around my innards."

A hard-learned lesson from a few months ago that had been fascinating to be a part of. Jessica had drunk deeply from a glass of orange juice at knitting, and her child had awoken with a deep and great vengeance. Tiffany had never felt a life inside another woman. A goat, yes, but that was so different. Jessica had guided Tiffany's hand onto her belly just as a hard kick made her grunt. Even now Tiffany could feel the memory of that tiny footprint upon her palm. It was surreal and miraculous, and had made them both smile at the time.

June 1900

> *Ernest, the ship's captain told me, has jumped ship in Eureka, which made little sense to me as it is not a normal port of call for the big lumber schooner. The First Mate, Albert Slater, later told me the truth. Ernest died in a brothel during a knife fight after beating a Chinese whore to death.*
>
> *So he has paid the price of his deeds as have I. I had thought that, at forty, I was long past conceiving…I am not.*
>
> *My daughter sends word by Albert—a far more trusty man than my Ernest it seems—that she had to miss this ship, but shall return upon the next to sail. It saddens me, for I miss her so.*
>
> *I would hate this child growing within me if I could, but such feelings I am unable to discover. I can only feel love for it.*
>
> *Though how to tell Pearl of her sibling to be, God alone knows.*

Tiffany looked at Jessica as she scowled down at her own bulging belly.

"You will take such joy in this child, Jessica. You will not be able to help yourself and you will guard her as you would no other, not your husband or even yourself." It was a direct quote, but for the name change, of Lillian's instructions to herself.

The only sound in the room was the distant rattle of the bottling machine in the back of the brewery, which was muffled by the glass-and-wood walls.

"Did you ever…" Jessica asked softly.

Tiffany pulled herself back. "No." She placed a hand on her own belly. "No. Though I have imagined it." So clearly described by Lillian Lamont. Tiffany felt it as if she had lived through an entire pregnancy herself—the joys and the fears.

Had her own mother hated Tiffany as she grew in the womb? Despised her for ruining her mother's figure? Her governess had told Tiffany years ago that she had not been nursed, even once, for fear of misshapen breasts.

Lillian Lamont had loved her children, both of them.

"You are a very strange woman, Tiffany," Jessica regarded her levelly.

Tiffany squirmed in her seat.

"I knew there was a reason I liked you."

Her tease startled Tiffany into looking back up at Jessica. "Takes one to know one, I suppose." And Tiffany could not believe the words that had just come out of her own mouth.

Natalya's laugh sounded first. As others joined in, Natalya winked at her and nodded that she too was a friend.

Tiffany's smile didn't feel tentative on her face as she winked back. Though conversation soon shifted to the next upcoming town festival, just two weeks off, Tiffany could feel the change. For perhaps the first time since her arrival in Eagle Cove, she didn't sit emotionally outside the circle while she physically sat within it. She belonged here. A surprising place where friends cared for her.

There was only one better feeling.

There was also a man waiting for her.

# # #

Devin sat on a handy log and Tall Guy sat on the ground beside him, which placed their heads at roughly the same height. The goats milled about nibbling at the flake of hay he had tossed down for them. Beth—at least he thought it was Beth—had, in her patient way, adopted Shprintze along with Chava. The orphaned kid was visibly thriving though she was less than a week old.

The afternoon was fading to evening but Tiffany wasn't here. He'd forgotten it was Tuesday. One of her knitting days. At least he'd showered off the day's work at the B&B before climbing the trail this time.

"A lot of fair ladies here," he told Tall Guy.

The dog studied him silently.

"Wrong species for either of us, I know." Then he felt bad because Tall Guy had no one of his own breed to be waiting for, whereas Tiffany would soon return.

Devin watched as one of goats lay down to rest and then one of the kids used her as a platform to leap for the log. A sharp bleat, first from the goat-as-launching-platform, then from the kid as it failed to achieve orbit, scrabbled briefly at the log's bark, then plopped down on the ground.

"I'm losing my mind. Do you know how many goats we have in all of Chicago? About twice as many as you guard, my friend. That's it. And they're all safely in the Lincoln Park petting zoo. You'd hate it there."

Tall Guy snuffled at his pockets again, but he had no dog biscuits. He didn't even know where Tiffany kept them, so he scratched the dog's ear, which was apparently a distant second as far as pleasures went, but was considered better than nothing.

Devin had been here for…he wasn't even sure. The days had already blurred together. And since he'd sent his phone to the bottom of the ocean to "sleep with the fishes" (nothing like a good *Godfather* quote), he'd lost track of time. He didn't miss his phone, not a bit. He'd used the B&B's phone to let his foreman know how to reach him, but he felt no desire to go and replace his electronic connection to the rest of the world. He had a tablet for e-mail, but ignored that as well. The company account messages were auto-copied to his foreman. The rest were all pieces of his past doing their best to yank him back to Chicago, to a life that now disgusted him.

Time moved differently here. Rather than over-scheduled crews and massive project deadlines on a dozen houses being built at once, he had a single project and one worker: himself.

And he had a girl. A woman.

"What am I doing?"

Tall Guy didn't have any idea either.

"You're no help at all."

The dog sighed.

Devin didn't love Tiffany. No exactly. Not so soon. But he… cared for her. The fact that he cared for her more than he ever had for Rebecca—to whom he had been misguided enough to declare his love—was all just one more sad reinforcement regarding his misspent youth. His utterly naive youth of two months ago.

One of the kids sidled over, thinking it was being very sly, and began to nibble on one of Devin's bootlaces.

"Fine. Do your worst."

The baby goat managed to get a good hold of one lace then tried to bolt away while still clamping onto it. In the middle of its first leap, it ran out of bootlace and tumbled to the ground. Then digging in all fours, it tugged and wrestled at it, jerking Devin's boot side to side.

"You'll never get that knot untied."

"I know," he told the dog. "It's like Eagle Cove is tying me up in all sorts of ways."

"It will do that."

Devin looked at Tall Guy. He hadn't said a word.

Then Tiffany held out a biscuit and Tall Guy sighed happily as he took it. He lay down and began crunching on it.

"Hi," was all Devin could manage, now as speechless as the big Kangal. Tiffany was dressed in a pretty blouse of summer-blue that the light wind pressed against her figure. Her jeans were worn soft enough to cling to every curve. There were shapes revealed that he was only starting to learn and definitely to appreciate.

But it wasn't her exceptional body or her amazing hair that stunned him speechless, it was the simple joy of her smile at finding him here. The bright sparkle in her blue-gray eyes.

He pulled her in until she was standing between his knees, where he could wrap his arms about her waist and rest his face between her breasts. She set her knitting bag and her bow on the log beside him and circled her arms about his head.

"The world is so quiet when you hold me," he told her.

"The world is so full for me when I do."

"Full of what?" He placed a kiss on her sternum as an excuse to not raise his head from where it rested in heaven.

"No. It doesn't work that way. It's just…full. As if, when I'm holding you, I don't need anything else. Couldn't need anything more."

Devin could tell that she was looking down at him by how her hair slid about his ears and neck. He was inside the shield, so close to Tiffany that everyone else couldn't help but be outside. He slipped his hands down until he was hugging her about the hips. The hips that welcomed him so deliciously. He locked his arms about her tighter and tighter as if he could find some way to hold on.

"I'm getting lost here, Tiffany."

"I don't see why," she began scratching his head lightly with her short, practical nails. "Tucked in between my breasts would seem like a 'found' place to me rather than a lost one."

He tipped his head up to look at her, her face mere inches above his. He sang the line from "Amazing Grace." "I once was lost, but now I'm found."

Tiffany picked up a sweet harmony that ended in one of her delightful giggles of joy. He'd never met someone so pleased with her life. And it showed on her face all the time.

"This is," he nuzzled back between her breasts, "a *very* found sort of place."

"Told you."

"Chicago isn't."

"Then don't think about it."

"Again that impossible simplicity you have. Your world is so clear. Mine is muddier than a construction site in a Chicago spring. We only have two seasons there, you know: winter and construction."

# # #

Tiffany laughed dutifully at his little joke, but her thoughts were whirling.

Her life was so clear? What wouldn't she give for that to be true.

"The two-season thing is especially true when you work for a major contractor," Devin continued talking to her breasts.

She'd always felt that men's fixation with breasts was a strange and ridiculous preoccupation. But for Devin, it was a place he changed. Something about resting his head there made him quiet and thoughtful. As close to peace as she ever saw him. He was good at having fun, far better than she was. But he never relaxed—she could feel his mind working ceaselessly.

With his head against her chest, whether after hot, sweaty lovemaking or as chastely as now, his thoughts went quiet. They moved more slowly. More peacefully.

Maybe her own life *was* clearer, at least when he was with her. The farm kept her busy. Her time occupied, but her thoughts free to lead her where they would. When Devin was with her, life seemed so right. That was it. Just…right.

She freed one hand and began unbuttoning her blouse. When she reached his face, he rolled his head aside onto her breast.

When she'd exposed a narrow cleavage down to her waist, she rocked his head back into place using the lightest of pressures.

With one strong arm, he kept her hips pulled hard against his chest. She leaned against him as he began to do more than merely rest his face against her skin. With no sense of shame at all, she rubbed against him, reveling in the slow build of heat. Let him expose her chest to the warmth of the setting sun.

The goats circled about them, like some distant parade. Their play appearing to be but a distant image. Their bleats barely louder than the roar of her own pulse and the gentle wind that cooled and teased.

Tiffany closed her eyes and let the sensations take her as he slowly made love to her.

Devin was right after all. Her life had never been so clear as this moment.

# # #

Devin slipped away at first light. He didn't go far, just to the edge of Tiffany's yurt deck. He wanted to see the land, watch it come awake. The night chill was still on the air but he'd grabbed a comforter off the back of the couch and wrapped it around him.

A family of deer slept in the narrow passage between the forest and Tiffany's vegetable garden fence just a few dozen feet away. He'd never seen them so close except in a zoo. They slept lying down, but with their heads up like a submarine periscope, wary of intruders. Only the delicate spotted fawn had lain down its head and given itself up to sleep with total abandon. Safe in the protection of its parents.

"It's cold out here," Tiffany scooted under the comforter with him. A deer ear swiveled to track her, but apparently she wasn't worrisome enough to make them wake all the way up and stand. Though, in sweatpants and a thick cable-knit sweater with a V-neck that revealed she wore nothing beneath it, Tiffany was very worth looking at in Devin's book. She was warm and sleep rumpled. And sex rumpled. He could never tire of the way she gave, with absolute abandon to her own emotions. Nor of the way she inspired him to return the favor. He kissed her briefly, but she pulled away.

"Eww! I have morning breath."

"Don't care. I bet I do too. Still don't care."

"I do. Besides, if I let you kiss me, I'll miss the sunrise." The fact that they faced west, not east, didn't seem to be worth making a point about.

He nodded over toward the family of deer.

"Boris, Natasha, and Nell," she named them.

"*Bullwinkle*," Devin nodded, recognizing the reference. "And if the fawn had been a boy?"

"Dudley, of course."

Devin looked at the deer again. "Seems cruel to rescue poor Nell Fenwick from the evil Snidely Whiplash only to place her into the family of the villains. Though they don't look very evil."

"Neither were Boris and Natasha. They delighted in thinking they were, but they'll make good parents."

Unlike his own, or Tiffany's. He thought about the small bits and pieces she'd dropped. The stepfather who had obviously been the abuser. The mother who had let it happen and who Tiffany mentioned even less than he mentioned his own.

She pointed at a pair of large gray doves with black rings about their necks as they darted about together from one branch to the next and called Who-WHO-who-who.

"What kind of parents will we be?"

"You and I?" Tiffany sounded suddenly breathless.

"Yes. No. I mean—" Devin definitely wasn't awake yet. "I mean I assume…no. *Do* you want to have kids some day? Yourself?"

She smiled tolerantly at his mangling of the question, but nodded. "You?"

"I do. I really do. But I'm afraid that I'll be like my parents."

"Don't worry, you won't be. No more than I'll be like mine," Tiffany replied complacently.

"How can you know? What makes us any different than my parents or yours?"

"Because, like Boris and Natasha, we care. If you need proof, just look at my girls and boys."

Though the goat pen was a couple hundred feet away and still lost in morning shadows, there was no doubting the occupants' physical and mental well-being. They were a very happy family of goats and a dog.

Devin turned to look at Tiffany, huddled so deep into the blanket and so close against him for warmth that he could see little more than her hair and her temple—so he kissed it. She was a woman who cared with all of her generous heart. He pulled her mostly into his lap and she curled up against his chest.

"You, Tiffany Mills, will make an amazing mother." He could see it in her.

She leaned even harder against him for a moment under the blanket in thanks. "I have a great example."

"Your mother doesn't sound like such a great example."

"No," she agreed. "But my several times great-grandmother was an amazing woman. The more I can be like her, the better person I'll be."

Devin knew almost nothing about his great-grandparents, never mind any generations before that except that they had once been Irish Catholics fleeing the Great Famine of the late 1840s.

"There's one thing that Lillian Lamont discovered far too late in life."

"What's that?"

"Come back to bed and I'll show you."

"Maybe," he took advantage of the loose sweater to slide his hand underneath it and cradle a breast. "But maybe I can't wait that long."

"No," Tiffany's delighted giggle only encouraged him.

Her breath caught short and hard as he slid his hand down inside her sweatpants and cupped her.

"I'll freeze."

"I promise to keep you very warm."

She groaned as he began to massage her. The deer startled, quickly rose, and ran away.

Tiffany's reactions also rose quickly but she didn't attempt to run at all. Instead she delighted him as her gasps told him he was capable of doing some things very right.

Chapter 7

Tiffany sat on Mrs. Winslow's porch and watched the McCall's house across Shearwater Lane. Vincent was working in his garage/woodshop, finishing an ornate bedstead. He was the town's leading custom furniture maker.

After half an hour of her sitting and watching him shape and sand, he came over and asked if she needed anything, which was nice of him.

He was covered head to toe in sawdust, only the outlines of his safety goggles and dust mask were clean. It reminded her of Devin, coming to her covered in plaster dust. It also reminded her of the first time they had made love, lying beneath the first stars on her front deck. She fought the blush that was rising fast to her cheeks.

"I'm fine. I wanted to speak with Mrs. Winslow."

"She's usually home shortly after my wife and kids. The twins are in her class this year. Shouldn't be long now."

"I'll just wait then. Thank you."

"Sure I can't get you anything? A glass of water or something?"

"Would it be filled with sawdust?"

He laughed as he looked down at himself, "Near enough."

"I'll pass, thank you." She'd meant it seriously, but could now see how it sounded funny. Before Devin she might not have ever noticed.

"Good choice," he offered a cheery wave then re-crossed the street back to his woodworking.

What else was Devin changing about her?

Another week had gone by and she was no longer "in love" with him. She had begun to suspect that her ancestor had stopped short of where Tiffany was moving to. A week ago, if Devin had left, she too would have been "sore of heart." If Devin left now, she would be lost.

When they made love, it was like nothing she had experienced or imagined. There was a connection that emerged from somewhere deep within her and it wanted only one thing: him. But that wasn't even the important part of what was happening.

They made each other happy.

Merely being in his presence, even just thinking about him, made her day brighter and happier. And she could see the same in him.

But that had not been enough to save Lillian Lamont.

July 1900

My Pearl has returned to me, a mere shadow of her former self. Her pallor as pale as Chinese silk and she is so gaunt that a corset made her appear heavier of frame rather than lighter. My corset yet hid my condition though it will do so only a little longer.

After I transported her from the dock to our home and sequestered her, I asked after her ailment.

"I could find no trace of him," she wailed. "I stayed an extra month to search, fearing him injured or falsely imprisoned."

When I asked who, she replied, "My true love. My one and only."

I swear that I felt a chill in that moment. Three hundred thousand they say reside in the great city of San Francisco, yet I felt a chill.

"The father of my unborn child is gone. We were to be married. Oh, my beloved." And she wailed upon my breast.

My wonder at the prospect of a grandchild lasted only a moment. With her next words, she cut all the cords that bind my life together. "Tis the messenger you sent to me. My dearest Ernest is nowhere to be found."

The man is dead. Blessedly, none had been so cruel as to speak truth to the young woman seeking him. And the second child, which I had decided was to be the joy of my elder years, became sawdust and bitter medicine. My handsome lover was also my daughter's. And my own child would be sibling to both Pearl and to her own child.

A minivan drove up and pulled into the McCall driveway. Seven-year-old twins climbed out then rushed to their father. Like miniatures of their mother, they had matching brunette ponytails and sparkling blue eyes. It was an easy bet that by high school they would also have their mother's powerful curves. Or as Tiffany's mother would have said, "Hussy, bought and paid for." Though there was no more question that Dawn McCall's shape was authentic than her own mother's—for she and Tiffany could be twins but for their age and attitude.

Vincent had shed his dust mask and glasses and was dusting himself off with whacks of a clean towel. Soon the twins also had towels and were making a game of thwapping them against his pant legs, releasing great clouds of sawdust. Once the worst of it was gone, he hugged them both, then—rather than returning to his work—he sat down on a sawhorse. By their animated gestures, they must be retelling the events of their day though she could hear only the happiness of their tone, not their words.

When Dawn McCall approached, Vincent moved to one side and made a show of dusting off the other end of his sawhorse. Dawn sat, slipped a hand around her husband's waist despite the risk of getting dirty, and soon the four of them were highly animated.

Tiffany barely noticed the car that pulled into the driveway until Mrs. Winslow came along the front walk.

"They make a beautiful family, don't they?"

Tiffany could only sigh and nod. So much more than she had ever had.

"You are still a puzzle to me, Tiffany Mills. Are you here to finally unravel the mystery?"

She flinched. She'd completely forgotten about her unconsidered comment at the wedding and Mrs. Winslow's interest in it.

Mrs. Winslow sighed heavily at her response. "Then why the visit, girl?"

Tiffany looked up at her. The irritation was obvious, but Tiffany couldn't think about two things at once, especially not when one of them was so big.

"Ms. Mills?"

"How do you know?" She blurted it out before she could second-guess herself yet again. "Devin? Everything? How do you know when—" She couldn't continue.

Mrs. Winslow regarded her steadily for a long time before speaking. "You have walked all of the way from your farm on a Monday to ask me this."

She didn't make it a question so Tiffany didn't feel obliged to answer.

"Come in now and we'll have some tea." With no further words, she unlocked the front door and led the way in.

# # #

Devin had seen Tiffany quickly pass by from the second story window of the lightkeeper's cottage. He scraped himself enough to bleed, but was unable to open the window. Too many layers of paint in the track had sealed it shut. He'd had them all replaced except this one because they'd mis-shipped it and the replacement hadn't arrived yet.

By the time he was downstairs, she was gone and he couldn't follow her.

"Well, she's allowed a life as well," he told the main panel as he hooked in the last of the new wiring. He'd pushed hard this week to get it done so that he'd have more time for the extra finish work he was planning. Dragon Winslow had been right—the visit to Hector's boat gave him the interior design style that he'd been missing.

"It's not like we're living together," he mentioned to the plumbing as he set up the pressure test for the inspector, who had agreed to drive out to the coast this afternoon along with the electrical inspector. Of course he hadn't been sleeping at the B&B. Not when Tiffany so welcomed him to her bed. He packed in some groceries and one night won her undying appreciation by delivering a Carrier Pigeon pizza. It had cooled on the hike in, but her oven had reheated it fast enough to not make him feel guilty about propane usage. Unsure what she liked, he'd made it half Hawaiian and half loaded. She'd taken a slice of each and, for New York-style pizza, it hadn't been half bad.

If he stayed here, he'd have to talk to them about offering some Chicago-style as well.

"If I stay here?" There was as unlikely an idea as he'd ever had. He made sure that he had the permits on display. "We're just—"

"Talking to ourselves."

"Oh. Hi, Peggy. What are you doing up here?"

"Thought I'd come see how you're doing. I take it that talking to yourself is a good sign?"

He smiled. "I'm used to working with a large crew. Seems awfully quiet if I don't."

He noticed the way she was looking at his work with more than just a casual eye.

"You know construction?" Then wished he could take it back. She owned a road grader, ran the airport, rebuilt airplanes… "Wait a minute."

She waited him out.

"You're married to Judge Slater."

A nod.

"But Slater isn't your last name."

"It is now. He's still old-fashioned enough to want his wife to take his last name. I didn't see any point in arguing."

"But that was recent."

Again the nod.

"What was your maiden name?"

"Naron."

Devin was standing right next to the permits where he'd nailed them to a stud, but he didn't need look at them; the last name of the contractor who'd arranged the permit for him to work under started with an N. "You're Eagle Cove Contracting."

She shrugged as if it shouldn't be a surprise. "I've done a lot of building in this town."

In Chicago, getting a woman on the crew was such a rarity that she was still often razzed or even harassed until she left. Devin was proud of his D.R. crew because they had two women who insisted they were treated fine whenever he checked in with them.

In Eagle Cove, the main contractor in town was a woman.

"Huh," was all he managed. He made a mental gear shift, hard enough to do some grinding inside his skull. So she was here to make sure that his work was up to whatever standards Eagle Cove Contracting was known for. Because it was Peggy, he now knew that her standards were sky high. And the fact that she hadn't bothered to come by until shortly before the inspectors' planned arrival said something of what she thought of his skills.

"Well," he waved as casually as he could toward the rest of the interior, "let me know if you find anything. Inspectors are due any time."

Without a word, she turned and began walking through the cottage, doing her own pre-inspection inspection. He'd stripped the inside walls down to stud as well, so he could see her moving about. It felt as if someone was silently peeking inside his head to make sure his brain was still operating properly. She took more time than any self-respecting building inspector ever would.

She went upstairs and he resisted the urge to follow though he certainly traced her steps back and forth across the ceiling. When she returned, he realized that he hadn't moved an inch from standing in front of the permits, like some kind of a wind-up doll that someone had cranked full tight and had forgotten to hit the release switch.

"Why not fur out the old two-by-four walls to two-by-six so that you can fit R-21 insulation batts?"

"I'm going to do a closed-cell polyurethane. I didn't want to steal space as the rooms are already small. I'll get the same insulation factor and it doesn't get cold enough here to justify the expense and loss of interior space to push up to R-33. In Chicago, different answer."

"Doing it yourself?"

"Could, except my equipment is in Chicago. Subbing it out."

"To Gregor?"

At his confirmation, she nodded.

"What about sound insulation between rooms?"

"Standoffs and more spray-in foam, open-cell. Guests want their privacy in a romantic getaway but there's no need to waste money on an R-value we don't need."

She never once turned or pointed, demonstrating that she'd absolutely seen every single thing she'd looked at. "Second floor, third stud in the back bath has an age split. You'll need to sister on a new board."

He'd spotted that, but hadn't gotten to it yet.

He had seven items by the time the inspectors' arrival finally rescued him. Was that good, a nice short list? Or bad? He couldn't read Peggy well enough to tell. They were all minor items and not a one would concern an inspector, as none were structural.

Despite their long drive down from Newport, the inspectors completed their inspection in well under half an hour. Devin had the feeling that it had less to do with his workmanship and far more to do with Peggy's presence and her name on the permit.

"See ya', Peg," and they were gone again.

Both permits were signed, "Okay to insulate."

"Wait!" Devin stepped outside but they were gone.

Peggy joined him. "What's the problem?"

"They also signed 'Okay to cover.' I haven't insulated yet and they need to inspect that once it's in."

"John's also a building inspector for remote locales like Eagle Cove. He knows that I'll kick your ass if you don't do a good job. Saves him a trip."

"Oh." Devin blinked at the bright day. The interior of the cottage was relatively dim through the smaller style of windows prevalent a hundred years ago. "Are you going to kick my ass?"

"Nope," Peggy stuck her hands in her pockets. "Nice work."

"Uh, thanks." She'd proven that she expected the same standards of work he did from his own crew and it felt good to find another contractor who truly cared about the quality of work. He handed her a water bottle and took another himself from the cooler he kept in the back of his truck.

"Now what's this about you living up at Tiffany's?"

Devin was glad he hadn't opened his water yet or he'd be choking on it.

# # #

Tiffany was surprised that Mrs. Winslow understood the peace that making tea deserved. There should be some rituals that are sacrosanct and Tiffany had always enjoyed the process making a pot of tea. Preheating the pot with a swirl of boiling water. Loose tea leaves, then a tea cozy to retain the heat while it steeped.

Mrs. Winslow's cozy was simple, attractive…and tea-colored.

Tiffany's first one had been a nice bit of cable-knit wool, in the purest white. In days it had been stained with brown splashes of tea. It had gotten uglier and uglier until she'd had the idea of doing a tea-leaf dye bath. The white wool cozy had come out nicely tea-toned and she still used it every morning. They carried the tea service out into the backyard.

Mrs. Winslow's back garden was a lush wonder.

Tiffany's gardens were a study in the practical and the robust. Much of her food came from the garden, and it had to be strong enough to thrive despite the massive winds that occasionally slammed into the high ridge. A smaller seventy- or eighty-mile-an-hour wind down in Eagle Cove could easily top a hundred on her anemometer there above the headland. When those big storms arrived, the yurt's fabric flexed and slapped, making it impossible to sleep even by wearing earplugs…one of the only drawbacks to her home.

Mrs. Winslow's garden included a tiny herb bed and not another practical plant in the whole lot. Late tulips and early roses. Snapdragons teased peonies. Freesia borders accented Gerbera daisies.

And it was filled with bird life. Hummingbirds sipped sugar water from floral feeders. Stellar jays, chickadees, and red-winged blackbirds abounded at seed and suet feeders.

"Fairyland," Tiffany kept turning about, trying to take it all in. She needed to build a place where she could do this. "It's magical."

"Thank you, Ms. Mills."

"Is it okay if I never leave?"

"I am glad that you appreciate it. You are always welcome in my garden, Ms. Mills."

Mrs. Winslow didn't make it sound like an empty offer and Tiffany retreated into silence.

When the tea was brewed, Tiffany poured while Mrs. Winslow went inside and returned with a plate of cookies. "Scottish shortbread. One of my weaknesses that I indulge in only on special occasions."

"Special occasions?" And Tiffany's nerves shot to life once more. Suddenly she wished she'd never come. She knew that, after Mrs. Winslow's kindness, there was no way that she could avoid revealing Lillian Lamont's story. And when she did, her own life would so pale in comparison. Lillian had founded a town and a matriarchy—two of them actually, here and in San Francisco—Tiffany had founded a farm with six goats. And the truth of her heritage would come out and her connection to—

"Yes," Mrs. Winslow studied her closely. "It is not often you fall in love."

Tiffany attempted to breathe but wasn't having much luck with it. Okay, even scarier than any revelation of her past was that simple, yet ever so true, statement of her present.

# # #

Devin sat down abruptly on the lumber he'd stacked up to build the roof over the porch.

"I'm not living with her."

"Oh." Peggy sat opposite him on a large rock he'd nudged into place using the grader. A nice big boulder, it made a statement close beside the front door. "What do they call it these days?"

"You're not helping."

"Wasn't trying to."

"Great. What are you trying to do?"

Peggy kicked at the dirt a bit before answering. "Some people in this town are mighty protective of that girl."

"I'm one of them."

Peggy nodded without looking up. "Thought so. Anyone harasses you about that…"

"Then…" he prompted when she didn't continue.

"Then," she finally looked up at him. Her blue eyes were suddenly hard as steel. "Tell 'em to go fuck themselves. It's between you and her."

He sipped at his water while he considered his next words. "Peggy?"

"Uh-huh."

"If you're ever in Chicago looking for work, I can always use a good crew boss."

"Ha!" It was a single short bark of laughter. Then she stood and pulled her gloves out of her back pocket. "I've got the last replacement window in my truck; just came in."

"I'll do the list and then I'll meet you there."

They finished their water bottles, chucked the empties into his truck bed in unison, and headed back inside to finish the prep work for the insulation.

# # #

Tiffany wished she could argue, but being in love was exactly the problem. Being really in love. She deeply feared that Lillian Lamont had only experienced true lust. And while it had clearly been joyous based upon her entries, it now left Tiffany wholly adrift without any clear guidance of how to be.

"Why come to me? What about your friends?"

"*You* are my first friend in Eagle Cove, Mrs. Wilson."

"Oh damn, child."

Tiffany looked up to see her wiping at her eyes.

"That… Oh dear." She blew her nose into a paper napkin and then reached across the small table to squeeze Tiffany's hand. "Well, if we are such great friends, Ms. Mills, then you had best call me Maggie and I shall call you Tiffany, henceforth."

"Okay, Maggie," Tiffany stumbled a bit over it. Because she'd almost said…well, why not? "Unless Dragon Maggie would be better?"

And Maggie let loose a big laugh that would fit a woman three times her size. "Oh, there's hope for you yet, Tiffany. There's hope for you yet."

Tiffany was surprised. She'd driven Maggie Winslow to contractions—a rare event indeed.

"Seriously though. What about your friends?"

Tiffany considered her teacup, turning it around several times on the saucer. Jessica, Becky, and Natalya. "They're all recently married. I'm not saying that's a bad thing, but I expect that their perspective is that everyone should be as happily married as they are and the sooner the better. I suppose it's a lot like how it must be for you watching Peggy Slater and Gina Lamont's recent weddings."

"Hmm," it sounded distinctly like a dragony growl of dissatisfaction with Tiffany's statement. "And that is not your perspective?"

"I have reasons to be careful. And cautious."

"Which of those are you going to explain first?"

Tiffany half wished she was speaking with someone far less perceptive, but then again, that's why she'd come to Mrs.—to Maggie. She needed a sounding board.

And Maggie waited patiently.

"Cautious," Tiffany decided. "My past relationships have rarely been…pleasant."

"Did you make them pay for what they did to you?" The Dragon was suddenly at the forefront.

Tiffany didn't like to think of it so bluntly, but she had and finally nodded.

"Good! There were events in my life…but those were different times. Or so I thought then…. Now I am less sure. And your present relationship?" She made it sound like a threat to commit mayhem on behalf of all women everywhere.

"He's glorious!" Tiffany assured her. "Devin is the most wonderful man who has—" And she realized that she was effusing. She took a deep breath, which almost turned into an incipient hiccup, but she managed to defeat it by exhaling slowly. She was ridiculous when she got the hiccups; her hair flounced in all directions with each attack.

Maggie was smiling at her.

"He's better than anything I ever dreamed of."

"Thing?" The second-grade schoolteacher tone was unmistakable.

"One. Any*one*."

"Then what is the problem?"

"How do you *know*?"

"That you are in love?" Maggie shrugged. "I married a good man. We were compatible for over thirty years until he passed. Gave me two sons whom I love very much. But was I ever 'in love' with him? I do not know, which perhaps answers the question itself."

"But Hector?"

And Maggie sighed. "Next you will have *me* asking *you* 'How do you know?' I would much prefer to not consider such eventualities."

"The lady doth protest too much, methinks."

And the two of them shared a laugh as they turned back to watch the birds flit about the lush garden.

Because Tiffany had learned one thing: they were both ladies who already knew.

The rest of the afternoon passed quietly before Mrs. Winslow gave her a ride back up to the lighthouse meadow. Devin's truck was parked there, but there was no sign of him, which told her that he was already up at the farm.

Thankfully, her friend Maggie never asked about the second half: why Tiffany also had to be so careful in addition to being cautious.

Chapter 8

"D evin!" *Gina flagged him* down as he drove by the B&B.

He stopped and climbed out of the truck as she swooped down the front stairs. He'd learned, in a small town, there was always time. In Chicago he wouldn't have bothered to exit the truck or even shut down the engine. Here such an action might not be actively rude, but it wasn't exactly sociable either.

"I tried calling you." Gina was a very fine-looking woman, but she was practically glowing this morning.

"You're looking good, Ms. Lamont. Like marriage really agrees with you."

"You have *no* idea. Neither did I. It took me until I was past fifty to find the right man, but oh did I ever," and her smile spoke sufficient volumes for Devin to feel a bit voyeuristic.

"I heaved my phone into the ocean," he told her. "I haven't missed it enough to replace it yet." Which was actually surprising as hell. In Chicago, if he was disconnected for even an hour, he'd worry about what he was missing.

Gina held up a hand and he high-fived it. "Welcome to the coast, Devin."

"Thanks. I think."

"I don't suppose Tiffany has a phone," there was some tease in her voice, but it was friendly rather than judgmental.

"I doubt it. I certainly haven't seen one. She'd have even less use for it than I do."

"Thought as much," Gina leaned back against his truck hood and raised her face into the morning sunlight.

He leaned beside her and did the same. It was late April. Back in Chicago it could be cold-snapping down to the teens, or baking into the eighties. Here it was late morning, so the air was mid-fifties and so fresh he felt better just for breathing it. The sun was different here. He'd never believed that…Monet returning time and time again to Liguria, Italy because the light was so special there. But it was true. The Oregon sun was a kinder, gentler light than the Chicago one. There it was all glare and brightness, hard as a slap. Here it was warm and pleasant, then as often as not, slipping behind cloud or tree branch to leave a cool caress when a breeze slid by.

"Are you busy at the moment?"

He shrugged, "Not really. You probably saw the insulator's truck arrive this morning. Tomorrow I have the Sheetrockers in. I've finished the concrete pour for the front porch, but I'd just be in everyone's way if I framed it up now. What do you need?"

"Not me. I'm all set for the festival, but Peggy could use a hand out at the airport."

"Festival?" He'd heard something about a festival as he passed through town on errands, but between the renovation and Tiffany, he didn't slow down often…not even this much. After a month his thoughts might be shifting to Eagle Cove Time, but his body was still clearly on the Chicago clock. Now that he thought about it, that was another thing he should heave overboard…at least for as long as he was here.

"Flameagle Days," Gina didn't look down from the sun. "Jessica's fourth festival. She became the town's marketing manager nine months ago."

"And pregnant eight and a half ago."

"The two are definitely related, but that's a story for another time. This town wasn't dying, but it was fading. She planned a big festival every three months along with other advertising campaigns. We're financially healthier in the last year than in the prior thirty and it's all that girl's doing. This is her fourth one and no one except her knows what all of the pieces are."

"What in the world is a flameagle? A flaming eagle, like Burning Man in Nevada?"

"Nope. You'll see. Go help Peggy. And I'll expect you and Tiffany to be at the festival, not hiding up in your woods." Gina pushed off the truck and headed back to the B&B. "It's only Tuesday and we're already full. That Jessica is a marketing wizard."

Devin sat there a while longer, watching the sun climb up through the branches.

You and Tiffany.

Your woods.

He didn't know which was stranger. Hearing it stated as simple fact or that it was true. A month ago, the woods had been a strange and creepy place. It now seemed perfectly normal to wander up into the trees after work rather than head down to the B&B. Sometimes Tiffany would walk down to meet him and they'd walk together, holding hands where the trail was wide enough.

They'd greet Tall Guy, check the goats, shower together, cook, and make love. She had no television, so they often talked, read aloud to each other, or sometimes just wrapped up under a comforter on the porch and watched the sun set and the stars come out. He'd brought his guitar up from the B&B and they would often spend the evening serenading Tall Guy and the goats. Occasionally Jake would perch in the nearest fir and look down at them like they were insane, which was a point he wasn't going to argue. Insanely happy.

Devin no longer went out and hit the bar with his crew. No formal dinners at his house or Rebecca's, no social events that, in retrospect, had simply been what he was supposed to do. He'd never thought before about what he *wanted* to do. D.R. Builders was his, but after-hours his lifestyle had been dictated by default, not preference.

The image of strolling through some small-town fair with Tiffany at his side…that wouldn't be default. That would be his and hers.

Your woods.

You and Tiffany.

He knew they were a couple. "An item." He just wasn't sure when it had happened because it had been the most natural thing in the world since that first moment. He'd arrived at a wedding and a nameless woman with amazing hair and an incredible smile had taken his hand to lead him through the crowd.

Devin was smiling himself as he climbed back into his truck and headed for the airport. He didn't know where the future lay, but the present was pretty damned amazing.

# # #

"Your mother is looking for you," Tiffany's lawyer said on the satellite phone.

"Tell her no!" She felt sick to her stomach and was glad that Devin wasn't here to see how weak she really was.

"I already did." But there was something in Joel Masterson's voice that told her there was more.

"Why is she looking for me?"

"You recall that she does this every few years."

"Yes," Tiffany did, now that she was getting through the initial panic. "Is there something different about this time?"

"I don't think so…" again that hesitation. Joel was a cutthroat legal shark, one of the reasons she had hired him. It wasn't like him to avoid an issue.

"Joel?"

He sighed. "Ms. Mills. You and I go back well over a decade."

Joel had made his reputation in putting her prominent stepfather behind bars for abusing his teenage stepchild. That one case had led him to be a leading champion of individual women's rights—a very successful one.

"It isn't my place, but have you considered speaking with your mother?"

Tiffany could only manage a strangled sound.

"Hear me out on this. You have escaped her. Run far, and by the sound of it, made good your choices."

Tiffany could only give him silence, but she was listening and he eventually continued.

"I will support whatever decision you make, Ms. Mills. But even your reaction now tells me that you are still running from her. That is not a life, Ms. Mills."

After another stretch of silence, he read off a cell phone number, which she dutifully wrote down.

"I apologize if I have crossed some line, Ms. Mills."

"No," she managed. "I don't think so. I just don't know if I'm brave enough to do this."

"If I may say, Tiffany?" It was the first time she could recall that he'd used her first name in all the years. "Your bravery is not in question here. Neither in confronting your stepfather in court, nor in choosing your own life, nor in building and running a farm yourself. None of those are the actions of the meek. I can only hope that someday you meet a man your age rather than mine who can see and appreciate that."

She thought about that a long time. "Maybe I already have, Joel."

"That, Ms. Mills, is the best news you have ever given me. As always, please call if I may be of any assistance." And he was gone.

# # #

"You want me to bale hay?" Devin tried not to feel too surprised. "I've never run a baler before."

"You'll learn," Peggy led him over the mown fields filled with the cut, dried hay neatly piled in long rows. One whole side of the airport had been in hay. They then crossed over a fence heading toward Becky's big, hip roof barn-turned-brewery. It glared blindingly white in the well-risen sun.

"Isn't it early?" Though the cut hay on the ground looked dry and rustled when he stepped on it.

"Wet winter, warm spring, and a drier than normal April. It's mature enough," she kicked at a windrow as they stepped over it. "I'd like to have let it grow another few weeks, but I don't trust Jessica."

"You don't trust her…to do what?" Devin couldn't imagine how not trusting a pregnant woman led to an early haying season.

"Her festival," Peggy raised a big bar on the front of the barn's massive main door.

"Flameagle Days. Gina mentioned that. What about it? What is a flameagle anyway?"

"My part of the festival is a fly-in. Pilots of small planes are always looking for a place to meet up. An event."

"Like a gathering of the Scottish clans. The Highland Games of flying?"

"Right. And Jessica is too good at her job. I expect the airport to get parked out and I'll have to overflow into this field. But I'm not willing to sacrifice the hay to her festival, so we have to take it in early."

Together they dragged the big doors aside and revealed a whole collection of strange machinery.

The barn itself had been partly converted to Becky's immaculate brewery, cordoned off behind wood-and-glass walls on this side just as it had been between her living area and the tasting room on the other side of the building. But part of it was still pure barn, with straw scattered on the packed-dirt floor and some elaborate examples of the steel fabricator's art into forms he couldn't begin to comprehend.

"Hay mower," Peggy rapped one as they passed by. "Hay rake for turning the drying hay and then gathering it into windrows," she pointed to another.

"Uh-huh," he did his best to make it sound as if he knew how these things worked, rather than wondering what medieval dungeon these torture devices had been stolen from.

"Blueberry picker."

That stopped him. "Blueberry picker?"

At a window, she pointed across the airfield that stretched alongside Becky's hay fields. On the far side of the airstrip was a vast field of white blossoms.

"Those are blueberry bushes?"

"Uh-huh."

"And this machine picks them?" It looked more as if it was designed to eat unwary cows, or maybe small elephants.

"Whatever the U-pickers don't harvest."

"Uh-huh." He tried to puzzle out how it could possibly do that when he was distracted by the last machine in the barn. It was bizarre enough for him to stop wondering why Gina had sent him to Peggy, who in turn was having Devin drive Becky's equipment to bale hay. Maybe that was just how small towns worked.

"Here it is."

He'd never driven a farm tractor, but that looked enough like other construction machinery that it didn't worry him.

The John Deere tractor was bright green. He supposed it was a little one, especially compared to the giants he'd seen at work out on the Great Plains as he drove through, but it was still a big machine.

But the contraption attached to the back of the tractor in Becky's barn was alarming. It was a strange, off-center device on two wheels. It had about a thousand, foot-long tines sticking out of a central drum. They must sweep the hay up and then do mysterious things with it inside the rest of the blocky machine.

Peggy led him back, pointing out how to restock bailing twine and where the bales were ejected. Ejected was the right word. The last item in the Rube Goldberg train of equipment was a big cart with wood slat sides. It had definitely been used hard.

"The baler will loft the finished bale into the cart, so don't turn too sharply at the end of the row or it may loft it over the side."

"Don't you have a floor I can sweep instead?"

"I was going to do this myself," Peggy grinned at him. "But that damn Jessica. She may be as big as a hay bale herself, but she knows her marketing. I have a half-dozen flights booked already today and the festival is still four days off. I need this field clear by then." She clapped him hard on the shoulder. "Good luck!"

And she left him. He could tell by her saunter on her way back over the fields to the airport that she was really enjoying leaving him to figure this all out himself. Well, he wasn't scared by the challenge. He was going to take it head-on. After all, he was a Grader Master.

Then he turned to look at the controls and felt much less comfortable with that decision.

"I don't even know how to…" And he stopped himself.

Some forever time ago he'd said those same words to Tiffany back before he earned his Grader Mastership. He'd hated that machine at first, but now it would always have a soft place in his heart. It was the first place he'd ever kissed her—an event that might not be changing his life, but it had certainly changed his summer.

Actually. His life was changing too, he just wasn't sure how.

"Okay," he told the tractor. "You don't scare me," which was only half a lie. On both counts: tractor and mysteriously changing life.

I think, he could almost imagine Tiffany standing beside him, *you should teach me how to use this.*

He'd pretend that she was talking about the tractor and not the life.

And so he did. He went over each control and explained it aloud until he was sure that he understood it. When he was done, he started the tractor and put on his sunglasses before pulling out of the barn.

Then he let out the clutch.

The tractor jolted backward, which shoved against the baler, turning it cockeyed as it jammed against the catcher cart. Then he stalled the engine in his attempt to recover.

He was glad that Tiffany wasn't there to see him; she'd be laughing herself to death in that merry way of hers.

Then Devin turned and saw that someone else was. Inside the brewery, Becky was standing at the window as if she'd been watching him a long time. Though he couldn't hear her, it was easy to see that she was howling with laughter.

Devin turned away, restarted the tractor, and eased forward out of the barn.

# # #

Tiffany stood at the edge of the field and watched Devin baling hay. He looked as if he'd done it forever. He sat just slightly sideways in the seat, often casting an eye back to make sure everything was in order. Every twenty seconds, the baler lofted a fifty-pound cube of hay high into the air where it tumbled into the cart being towed behind. Everything was as it should be, except the madness in her head.

Three years ago she had learned to enjoy the long walks to town as a time of peace and quiet in her day. For the first time, she had been in such a hurry to find Devin that she had come down the back logging road from her property, cutting the four-mile walk to two, and still she was a little breathless from how fast she'd traveled.

But watching Devin, suddenly her world was at peace again. Everything was where it should be.

Almost everything.

He spotted her, though she had stayed in the shade of the trees at the far end of the field. With a wave, he called her to him and her feet were in motion before she had a chance to decide. The tractor was moving so slowly that it was easy to time her steps. She arrived at the end of a windrow at the same moment as the tractor, grabbed a handrail, and stepped up the short ladder without Devin having to even slow the machine.

"Hi!" He kissed her quickly, then turned to check on his progress. "Aren't you early for knitting?"

Tuesday. She'd completely forgotten it was Tuesday. A glance skyward showed that it was still morning, but it would be a long day by the time she walked home to fetch her knitting and walk all the way back.

Then he turned from his baling to look at her once more. His smile faded as he squinted at her face a moment. Without saying anything else, he stopped the tractor and cycled down the machinery. She could hear him talking to himself as he did it. "Once we stop, we shift into neutral. Ease the engine down to idle. Now, disconnect the PTO to stop the baler…"

Just like the road grader. It was charming to think that in a way she had been with him all morning even though they had been in separate places. But it didn't make her feel any better about the phone call.

When finally everything was shut off and the only sounds were soft birdcall and the distant roar of Peggy's Stearman 4 biplane soaring high above, Devin pulled her into his lap.

"What's wrong?"

"Did I—" No. With Devin she didn't need to say when something was wrong. He would simply know. "I—" but she wasn't having any better luck without the "did."

Jake swooped close by the tractor and landed fast in the field less than a dozen feet away. A moment later he was back aloft with a vole or something in his claws. At least she was fairly sure it was Jake, but he'd finished his molt and now looked like any other bald eagle—huge and dangerous.

"Way to go, Jake," Devin whispered. He'd come a long way from diving out of the road grader in panic when an eagle flew by.

"Do you love me?" She blurted it out. "Sorry, that's not at all the question I rehearsed all the way here. That was unfair of me to—"

"Yes."

She stopped and looked at him. "Yes? Just yes?"

"Just yes," he nodded. "Like you just said, not the answer I expected to give at all. But it's the one that came out."

Then he grimaced and she feared he was regretting it already.

"Not exactly the most romantic way to say it. Sorry. I'll have to work on that before we get anywhere near to a proposal," he grimaced again. "And I did not just say that either. I—"

She kissed him and then burst into giggles that were really unbecoming on a woman who had just been told she was loved by someone who meant it.

Once they had both calmed down, she tried again.

"I have to do something awful."

"Why doesn't this sound good?"

"Because I just told you it will be awful."

"Okay," Devin kept his hands tight about her waist. "Would you care to define 'it' or should I start guessing? You have to cut your hair—which I should warn you would make me weep. You have amazing hair." He began toying with an end of it.

She shook her head and then had to dig a handful of it aside so that she could see him. Before she could speak, he continued.

"You have decided to give up the harp in favor of the harpsichord and you will make me follow you about the world carrying it on my back from one concert to the next."

Tiffany laid a hand over his mouth to stop him, but could feel his smile against her palm.

"I think I have to call my mother."

And she could feel the smile go away.

# # #

Devin felt as if he'd just stepped onto hot coals. One false move and the Tiffany-who-ran just might reemerge. Then he took some hope in that she'd *come* to him.

"You've been very careful to never mention her."

"You told me not to think about my past, so I haven't. Or very little."

He decided it wasn't simplicity that made her speak this way sometimes, nor was it some complex set of defense mechanisms. Devin thought back to a few nights before when they had been lying together in bed, watching the light of the moon that shone through the yurt's clear dome slowly sweep across the room.

"It's like a celestial searchlight," Tiffany had whispered in awe.

It had reminded him of the searchlights at the party for CMC's latest skyscraper. They had lit up the sky in celebration. Reds, blues, and golds of the CMC logo sweeping over the eighty stories of modernist glass and steel. The D.R. Builders' colors would not translate so well, a pale blue and a—

"Pudding!" Tiffany had exclaimed from beside him.

"What?"

"I just remembered that we have some chocolate pudding. Do you want some?" And already she was up and walking naked through the patch of moonlight, lit up like a magical elf.

"What were you thinking about?" He'd been trying to understand how she got from moon to pudding.

"When?" She opened the refrigerator and the white glow turned her skin from shadowed bronze to blinding alabaster.

"Before the pudding."

"I was thinking about the moonlight."

"What about it?"

"Nothing. I was just watching the light."

And now, sitting on the tractor with Tiffany in his lap, he finally understood. Her mind wasn't simple, it was just a much more peaceful place than his. She had been thinking about the moonlight and then she had thought of pudding.

He'd told her *not* to think about the past, and he'd wager that, for the most part, she hadn't.

Whereas he was *still* replaying Rebecca's phone call in his mind. Which in turn made him wonder how long she'd kept talking after the phone sank. Also how deep the phone had sunk before it shorted out. Or had some component been crushed first by the increasing pressure as it went deeper. And—

"Pudding," he said to her.

"No, mother."

He waited a beat and then she burst out laughing.

"You're still thinking about the pudding?"

"Well, that and how amazing you looked as you walked naked through the moonlight to bring it back to bed."

"Your mind is a very strange place, Devin Robison."

"And yours isn't, Tiffany Mills?"

She closed her eyes for a long moment and when she opened them the earlier sadness had returned.

He kept his hands firmly on her waist in case she tried to flee.

"My name isn't Tiffany Mills."

"Your name could be Lizzie Borden and I wouldn't care. Though I might hide all the axes."

"My name isn't Lizzie either." No tease. Ms. Forthright once again.

"Sooo…" he prompted her.

"Oh. My name is Tiffany Lamont."

"Well at least I had it half right. Tiffany—wait a sec. Lamont? Like Gina Lamont?"

"Yes."

"Is she your mother? She doesn't act like she knows. Are you some long-lost adopted child or—" Devin finally shut up, having learned that Tiffany needed the room of enough silence to speak.

"No. She's not my mother, my sister, nor my aunt. What matters is *my* mother—who isn't Gina. I think I have to call her."

"Well, Lamont sounds safer than Borden with her axe. Though if that makes you a relative of Natalya, maybe I'll just lay low."

He took a hand from her waist and held it out until she finally clasped it tentatively with her own. "Hello, Tiffany Lamont. I'm Devin Robison and I'm still in love with you. Wow! That does feel cool to say. Wait a sec—Tiffany…Lamont?"

She froze, her fingers somehow going cold though he still held onto them.

"San Francisco. You said you were from there. Some banker used to handle some of CMC's investments. He—" And Devin remembered. His father had told him the story one night over a bottle of Scotch about some brat stepkid destroying one of the best bankers ever, who had been put away then stabbed to death by another prisoner.

He was married to some high society bitch who got all his money in the bargain, his father had groaned at the injustice and freshened their Scotch glasses.

"You said your stepfather was killed," Devin was reaching for the rest of the memory.

Tiffany still didn't move. Her head remained bowed and her hair covered her face just as it had that first day when she was playing the harp.

Slowly, carefully, he brushed it back until he could see her face. "The San Francisco Lamonts as in Lamont Construction Supply and Shipping?"

Again no response. There simply weren't that many firms of the scale of CMC and LCSS in the country.

"Wow!"

And finally Tiffany flinched. Then she yanked her hand free of his. When he kept her in place, she began to struggle. He almost let her go, but then he remembered the haunted look on her face each time her family was mentioned—so he held on. It was time they got to the bottom of this.

She made fists, pounded them against his chest, and he wrapped his arms about her until she couldn't move. He'd never held a woman against her will. But this once, he *knew* it was the best choice.

"If you struggle any harder, you'll fall off my lap. It's a long way from a tractor seat to the ground."

"Damn you, let me go!"

So he did.

Caught by surprise, she remained on his lap though he knew it wouldn't last. So he confronted anger with anger.

"Do you think I give a rat's ass about who you were before I met you?"

She squinted at him. The mistrust lay clear upon her features—and it hurt like hell. But he knew that look. That fear. It was the same look he'd seen on his own face when he had realized why Rebecca Monica Monash had come after him. It was why he had never mentioned his father's name or CMC in Eagle Cove. Not in the interview with Gina and Cal, and not with Tiffany.

It all came down to money. And if she was from the LCSS lineage, she had plenty of it, too.

"Okay," Devin closed his eyes for a long moment. You didn't tell a woman you loved her and then keep secrets from her. And he'd done the first, so it was time to fix the second. "Tiffany."

It was strange to address her formally while she sat in his lap but in most ways was being very careful not to touch him. He forged on.

"You already know I'm about as smoothly romantic as a kumquat. So I'll say this straight. Next time you're on the Internet, look up the name of the CEO of Chicago Master Constructors."

# # #

Tiffany wondered if this was how the inside of Devin's head felt all the time. Hers felt as if it was going to explode as things shifted so rapidly and emotions slammed about so hard.

Trapped! She'd been so trapped. The feeling had been a slick, greasy shroud of horror.

Then he'd freed her the moment she asked and not struck. Not slapped. Not taken.

He had—kept her from her instinct to flee. No more. It didn't make the awful feeling go away, but he didn't repel her either.

Keeping a careful eye on him, she reached into her small backpack. She'd been out of the yurt and away before she'd discovered the satellite phone was still clenched in her hand. Now she pulled it out and hit last number redial.

"Hello?"

"Hi, Joel. Could you do me a favor and look up the last name of the CEO of CMC in Chicago?"

"Easy, Robison. It has been in the family for generations."

"And the son's name?"

"Heh!" It was the first time she'd ever heard anything close to a laugh from Joel Masterson. "Devin or Mikal? The former posted a nudie of his fiancéfiancée doing the latter almost at the altar. It went completely viral on the Internet. If you're talking about Mikal, he's harmless but a waste of time. Devin, though, is the heir apparent to the empire, though I hear he skipped town. He wrote something funny with the picture, but I can't remember what."

" 'I guess the wedding is off.' "

"That was it. Kid became a goddamn meme," Joel laughed aloud this time. "Supposed to be the merger of two empires, which the Monashs needed badly and the Robisons not so much. Are you okay?"

"I think so. I'll call you back and let you know."

"By end of day, Ms. Mills," Joel's voice was suddenly dead serious, "or I'm calling out the police."

"No need to bother him. It's a small town and Martin goes to bed early." And she hung up the phone.

Devin was still waiting for her reaction. Stone-faced, she could no longer see her lover in this careful man she was seated upon. She slipped off his lap but didn't climb down to the hay field.

"Did you say 'Wow!' because of my money?"

"No," Devin bit off the words as he spoke them. "I said that because Mills was so much easier to spell than Lamont. Did you screw me because of mine?"

Tiffany could only blink at him. This was all so messed up.

"Day one," he snapped out as if putting pieces together that didn't belong. "Chicago, contractor, and my name—my real name. Wouldn't have been hard to figure out with a quick search."

"I didn't. I swear, Devin, I didn't." She knew about the paranoia of money—knew how it attracted all the wrong type of attention. False friendship, insincere lovers, and worse. But there was no way that she could ever prove that wasn't her.

Defeated, she climbed down the tractor's ladder.

He jumped down and landed in front of her just as she reached the ground.

"Why did you change your name?" Again that unreadable, neutral voice that felt like a cold San Francisco fog. Or, a better analogy for him, a chilly wind off Lake Michigan.

"Do you know what rich boys do?" She practically shouted it out. She raised her hand to place it on his chest in apology, but instead let it drop. "*Some* rich boys?" She barely managed a whisper.

He waited in careful silence.

"They think they're god's gift," Tiffany explained. "And they think that once you've been abused that you must have wanted it. Then they—"

She could feel the chill of her shattering world as the shards of ice drove into her chest. How she—

And her face was crushed against Devin's chest before she even knew what happened.

"Aw, crap, Tiffany. I didn't know."

How would he? He was a good man.

"I hope to hell you got them all back but good."

"Most of them," she managed. Her nose was once again pressed into the same spot on his shoulder. This time, instead of muddy with plaster, he was going to make her sneeze with hay dust. She didn't care and managed to fight off the sneeze to stay in place. The tears were harder to fight, though she succeeded there as well.

But now what would he say? They both came from rich families, for all the good it had done them. Devin's parents weren't cruel, at least not intentionally like her stepfather. Would he speak first of wealth or of—

"Tell me why *we're* going to have to call your mother," he whispered in her ear.

Her heart was so smart; it had chosen to fall in love with a very good man. She pushed her face harder against his shoulder and breathed him in. Man, honest sweat, and—

Tiffany jerked back and unleashed a monstrous sneeze. Unable to raise her hands because he still held her so tightly, she splattered his shirt.

"Thorry," she managed with a sniffle. "You thmell like hay."

Then Devin laughed, which was the best sound in the world.

Chapter 9

Flameagle Days were in full swing and Tiffany was glad they had come, as long as Devin kept holding her hand when the crowds pressed too close. She and Devin had somehow managed to avoid being recruited for the weekend, perhaps because he'd done so much work leading up to the event.

They had tagged along on a bird watching tour, and Devin had made the whole crowd laugh when they'd oohed and aahed over seeing a bald eagle and Devin had called out, "His name is Jake."

Town smelled of strawberries. It seemed that every car had a couple flats of fresh-picked berries. Cal Jr. and Sr.'s Blackbird Bakery was selling strawberry-rhubarb pie and strawberry-custard tarts with a side of fresh-made vanilla ice cream as fast as they could dish it up.

She and Devin washed it down with a shared pint of Becky's Flameagle Stout.

And everywhere about town were the flameagles.

Jessica must have bought out the entire Oregon State supply of plastic flamingos. They had been painted brown, with white heads.

The metal sticks of their legs and their beaks had been painted yellow. Every eye was yellow with a black dot for the pupil, even the smallest ones. Some nested in planters of geraniums that decorated the main drag of Beach Way. Some had tiny knitted hats. Other, larger ones, cropped up in the strangest of places: in the trees, out on the beach, and especially out at the airport among the kajillion small planes that had flown in and filled the newly-hayed field.

"What's a flameagle's call?" Devin asked.

"Thock!" Tiffany declared.

"Thock?"

"They started life as plastic flamingos. Drop one on the floor. They go, 'Thock! Thock! Thock!' Each repeated call gets softer as they bounce."

"Okay, Ms. Know-it-all, what kind of eggs do they lay?"

"Very rare. They look just like Ping Pong balls."

He nodded, "That must be why they're endangered. Ping Pong players have been unwittingly harvesting them for years."

"Except in Eagle Cove," Tiffany corrected, for they were everywhere. And each had a number, as if they'd been tagged by a wildlife plasticologist. There were scavenger hunts for the most flameagles found, for finding the most that were a prime number, for finding the most that were still molting—identified by their speckled heads. Devin had spooked an enterprising group of teens who were going about with brown paint and a fine brush, speckling flameagle heads as they went.

She and Devin had finally wandered out to the airport, neither minding the long walk—which was good because driving was crazy in the packed small town.

There was an entire plane show going on in the field, like an antique car show. On the runway there were precision landing contests, hitting all wheels between two white lines just fifty feet apart—no bounces allowed.

"Flour-bombing," Devin observed and she followed where he was pointing. "Now that's a noble sport handed down from the times when men were men."

Devin was certainly a man. He was fun and funny, yet so male that she still was having trouble believing he was real.

Pilots flew over the field at five-hundred feet up and dropped tiny bags of flour, trying to "bomb" a giant tractor tire painted bright yellow and lying on the ground. Little splats of flour seemed to be everywhere about the field—except near the tire.

"Looks like fun," Devin was watching the planes avidly. "Care to be my bombardier next year?" It took one person to fly the plane safely and one to drop the flour bomb.

Tiffany was sure he wasn't aware of what he'd just said. He was leaving in three more months, at the end of the summer. His contract would be up when the lightkeeper's cottage was done and he'd be gone.

"Do you know how to fly?"

"I'll take lessons."

He still didn't get it and she did her best to ignore the pain. She couldn't follow him to Chicago. She had her farm, and deep connections to Eagle Cove—ones that she still hadn't told to anybody.

Then something happened. Planes scattered and it didn't take Tiffany long to see why. The ones they'd been watching were all propeller-driven planes. Some faster, some slower, and a few that looked to be plodding they moved so slowly, but they all used propellers.

Now a sleek business jet sliced through the sky, entered something Devin had called "the pattern," and dove for the field. She recognized the LCSS plane even before she saw the sailing ship logo. The Dassault Falcon 7x hit clean between the spot-landing contest stripes and decelerated with a massive roar of its triple jet engines, drowning then silencing all else on the field.

# # #

Devin could feel Tiffany's hand trembling in his and he squeezed it tightly.

The phone call had made this moment inevitable though it was still early on Sunday afternoon. The last events of the festival were still on-going and her mother wasn't supposed to arrive until after it was over. But it was too late to be helped.

He led her over to stand by the hangar as the private jet taxied up and stopped on the front apron—the paved area in front of the hangar. He didn't know what to expect when the ladder folded down, but still it was a shock.

An older version of Tiffany walked down the short set of stairs. She wore a designer dress more appropriate for a yachting party than an Eagle Cove fly-in and her hair was an elegant cut of the latest style. At least he imagined it was, because he could easily imagine it on his mother or Rebecca. The face was the same, the body shape, and oddly—the smile.

He'd expected it to be fake or studied or somehow plastic. But she looked actively happy to see her long-lost daughter.

"Oh, Lillian. This place? Really? After five generations you had to come back to Eagle Cove?" But Vivian Lamont's hug looked genuine and she held onto her daughter hard enough that it was clear that her daughter was more important than the neat-pressed lines of her designer sportswear.

Tiffany's face was to his side of her mother and he couldn't resist.

"You're Lillian now?" He whispered the question.

Tiffany sighed and nodded, still trapped in the hug. "I'm Lillian Tiffany Lamont."

"Why, of course you are." Her mother stepped back and did straighten out her dress.

The crowd that had gathered upon the jet's arrival slowly dispersed. Some to admire the jet, others to return their attention to the flour-bombing contest regaining its momentum.

"Of course she is," he agreed amiably. "Lillian," he couldn't resist the tease.

Tiffany started to wince at her name being different again, first Mills to Lamont and now…then he could see her catch on to his humor and shake her head ruefully at being caught again.

"Of course I am," she agreed with a smile.

"And who is this?" Tiffany's mother turned a discerning eye on him. He'd dressed in clean jeans and a nondescript button-down denim work shirt, Eagle Cove formal.

"This is Devin, Mother," and he could see Tiffany was trying to protect him by not even including his last name.

He looked at Vivian Lamont. He'd been prepared to hate her. He had reason to. How could she not have known that her husband was abusing her daughter? And wouldn't she have the same alley cat morals of his parents…and Rebecca's? And Rebecca.

But rather than being condescending, or attacking as if he was a gold-digger after Tiffany's money, he could see that she was putting the best face she could on a bundle of nerves.

Her daughter had rejected her a decade before in a desperate grab for self-preservation. But time had passed and now their future was dependent only on these two women—and Vivian *feared* her strong daughter's possible rejection, right down to her designer shoes. The media frenzy was gone, the bastard was dead, and life had moved on. Maybe, with a little help, they had a chance at finding at least friendship after all this time.

Devin took a careful breath, reassuring himself that there was no time like the present, and held out a hand.

"Devin Robison, Mrs. Lamont, of the Chicago Master Constructor Robisons. And I'm the one who is going to be marrying your daughter."

"You are?" The two of them said it in unison.

"Oh crap!" Devin turned to Tiffany. "I told you I was going to screw up the proposal."

She stepped forward into his arms and looked up at him. "No. You did it just great." Then she kissed him.

# # #

"Thank you all for coming to meet my mother," Tiffany was more than a little overwhelmed that they had.

She'd asked Devin and Maggie Winslow to meet her at Becky's brewery after the end of the Flameagle Days Festival. And that had necessitated asking Becky. Who in turn had invited Natalya and Jessica, who had brought their husbands and parents…so Gina, Cal Sr., Jessica's parents, and Judge and Peggy Slater were in attendance as well. Even Hector had docked from his last sailing charter to sit close beside Maggie.

Sixteen people—seventeen if she had counted herself but that number was entirely too big so she didn't. She hadn't addressed such a large crowd since mock-trials in law school.

It was a convivial group who had made her mother welcome and she would be forever grateful to them.

And her mother hadn't been merely gracious in return, she'd been…real. The way Tiffany had remembered her when still a child.

"I—" she looked at Devin in a plea for assistance.

He shot her a double thumbs up as if that helped anything.

"I'm not a good public speaker."

"You barely speak at all," Natalya corrected.

"Hush, Natya," Becky nodded to Tiffany. "You're doing great, Tiff. Rock on."

"You couldn't know, but my real name is—"

"Lillian," Maggie Winslow said in wonder.

"What?" Tiffany looked at her in surprise, but Maggie Winslow wasn't looking at her. She was looking up at the big mural above Becky's bar.

"You're the spitting image of Lillian Lamont."

"No way," Natalya protested. "I reproduced that from a historic photo."

Tiffany looked up at the painting. The two women there, dressed as Victorian ladies, didn't look anything alike. But the older one could have been Tiffany's twin. Right down to the long hair. A copy of the same photo had been in Lillian's journal and was the reason Tiffany had grown it out. She'd never noticed because it was a little too much like looking in the mirror.

"How is that possible?" Maggie pointed at the mural but was facing Tiffany.

Tiffany had known this moment was coming and knew she wouldn't have the nerves to tell the story herself. So she'd brought her four-times-great-grandmother's journal. Now she opened it and handed it to Devin who'd agreed to read the marked passage for her.

He rose to stand beside her and cleared his throat. The room went silent.

"This is the journal of Lillian Lamont," Devin began. "Tiffany's direct ancestor."

August 1900

I must leave this town and not return until my child is born. It can never be known to my dearest Pearl that she and I will give birth to half siblings, both sired by a dead man. I sail for San Francisco today. I cannot even bear to speak with her or see her for fear I will not have the strength to hold true to my purpose.

Devin turned to the next page she'd marked.

December 31, 1900

This year opened with a herald of such joy. My Pearl in her own home, preparing for a voyage that may yet cause Eagle Cove to thrive.

Now I am a woman in desperate fear of what has begun. I am old to bear a child, yet I would give anything but this unborn child's life if I could see my Pearl once more. I have prepared for every eventuality. Over my solicitor's protests, I have charged him with the care of my child should I not survive.

If my child lives, it shall have the San Francisco share and my beloved Pearl the Eagle Cove share of all we may achieve. As they are of near equal value, I have instructed him that this is to be done by severing the corporation into two separate entities so that neither child shall know of the other. Ever! However, if my child survives and is a girl, she and her descendants must always retain the Lamont name so that someday the breach may be sealed that lies beyond my power to repair.

"A different hand writes next," Devin's soft tone carried easily through the stilled room.

January 1, 1901

It is with saddened heart that I record the death this date of Lillian Lamont.

Yet with gladdened heart do I record the birth of Tiffany Lamont, so named by her mother from her deathbed.

He closed the journal softly and handed it back to her before sitting once more.

"I am named for both my ancestors, Lillian Tiffany Lamont. This," Tiffany squeezed the book hard, looking for strength, "I found this shelved in the family library when I was twelve and seeking an escape from…"

She saw her mother cower against the coming blow. They had spoken of it earlier, sitting quietly in the jet—Devin insisting that she was strong enough and must face this moment.

Sitting stone-faced in the luxurious leather, her mother had sworn that she didn't know. "Carl was always so charming. But there were certain events that he didn't care for, or so he said. No symphony or ballet for him, nor opera, nor social events with my friends—only with his. I now understand. I didn't then. I didn't even believe you when you charged him and they took away my husband. But I do now. I cannot beg forgiveness, not even from myself for being so blind, but I am so sorry for it."

Tiffany understood now that the stone-faced expression had been her mother's only place of safety in her ever so public life, trying to hide as desperately as Tiffany had in her woods. She nodded to her mother now. Perhaps Vivian could not forgive herself, but perhaps Tiffany could.

"This book helped me when I was seeking an escape from that period of my life," Tiffany explained to the waiting crowd, creating closure. She was now done with that.

Her mother began to silently cry, but they shared a tentative smile.

"This journal was unmarked on the binding and unre-membered for most of a century. It has been my keepsake, my strength, for many years."

She looked at Devin, who watched her with the warmest brown eyes and a rapt attention that she'd never dreamed of. He hadn't yet healed the breach between Tiffany and her mother, but he'd made it possible for her to imagine that it might someday be.

"I have found a new source of strength," she told the crowd but she saw only Devin and his confirming nod that he would be just that.

Then she stepped over to Maggie Winslow.

"You declared yourself the keeper of Eagle Cove's history. Here is the founding as told by a woman I have come to love very much." And she handed over the volume. It was like relinquishing herself, but it was also like freeing herself. She was no longer walking in Lillian Lamont's footsteps. From now on, she would walk in her own.

"You," Maggie whispered softly, "are the true keepsake."

Tiffany returned to Devin's side and sat beside him. She was exhausted by the sustained speech and by the emotions of the day. But laying her head on his shoulder, she knew that it didn't matter. As long as there were the two of them, somehow, somewhere together, it didn't matter.

Suddenly there was a commotion behind her and a scattering of the seats Becky had helped her gather together in the brewery.

A curse followed by Jessica crying out, "About time!"

Tiffany jolted up, clipping Devin's nose with the top of her head. She ignored him as he cried out and rushed to help. Jessica's water had broken and the first of her friends was finally having a baby.

Chapter 10

D*evin stood on the* yurt's deck and surveyed "their" domain. So much had changed from April to August.

For one, his wedding reception would be held in just a few hours at the two grand Victorian houses of Eagle Cove. They would be coming full circle, celebrating the first weekend of the Second Annual Puffin Days. Jessica's August festival had come around on the calendar once more. And before it truly began, there would a grand town party the likes of which Lillian and later Pearl Lamont had been known for before the Depression had struck. When it did, most of Pearl's fortune had gone into sustaining the town.

Everyone had agreed was totally appropriate as to make the reception so big because it was also the launch party for the book, *The Life and Loves of Lillian Lamont: an Oregon Pioneer's Journal (unabridged)*. The last point had included some hot debate, but Tiffany had been adamant that it was either her whole story or none of the story.

The next debate had been about the addendum co-written by Maggie and Jessica. Tiffany had won most of that one. Her own role in the entire history from Lillian's death to the present had been reduced to one small box on the "Genealogy of Lillian Lamont" page—with her name next to Devin's own (and today's ceremony would make that true). Jessica and Natalya were direct descendants of Pearl and, because Becky had married the other Slater brother, they were able to include her as well.

The farm was mentioned nowhere.

The book had been published on the town's behalf and the pre-orders were already several times bigger than the number of people who had ever lived in Eagle Cove—since its founding. Devin liked to think that was his doing, by suggesting that they include her first sexual encounter with Ernest as a teaser in the marketing.

For the big party, the Lamont B&B (which had descended through the direct line from Pearl) would be open. And the Judge had also opened his own neighboring house (that had been Lillian's before First Mate Albert Slater had purchased it after delivering the news of her death).

But the wedding itself was to be a small affair.

Devin had wanted it to be smaller by two people, just the original group that had sat in the brewery that night after the fly-in, but his fiancée had insisted. When he'd extended the final two invitations, he had told his parents that they were not allowed to sleep with anyone except each other for as long as they were both in Eagle Cove. They had eyed each other warily, but reserved only one room and with only one bed, so he had some hope.

The location was the second big change.

They were getting married on Tiffany's farm. It had started small, with a dinner invitation to Maggie and Hector. And once that had happened, Jessica, Natalya, and Becky had initiated an intense round of lobbying for a knitting session to be held at the yurt. And one fine June day, after three days spent in a mad flurry of preparation by the owner, her friends had come and had a wonderful time.

Now, the front deck of the yurt had been converted to an altar with the addition of a few rows of chairs. Both Judge Slaters were officiating, the retired judge as well as his son, Becky's husband Harry, who now served in his father's former seat. It was a dual wedding, but Tiffany and the Dragon had decided to make it a simultaneous ceremony and he and Hector were allowed no say in the matter.

Natasha, Becky, and Jessica—carrying her newborn Pearl, who looked just like her mother—had decided to stand for the women.

At something of a mutual loss, Hector and Devin had finally chosen Gina and Peggy to stand in the best-person roles to ensure that neither of them screwed up. In a last moment of inspiration, Devin had bribed Tall Guy to stand in as a third for the low price of just three dog biscuits.

Gina and Peggy had maintained the new Eagle Cove tradition and dressed in black for the ceremony. Gina looked as exotic and vivacious as ever, but Peggy was a complete surprise. She might still walk like she was out to conquer the Earth singlehandedly, but freed of her battered jeans and flannel work shirt, she was causing her husband the Judge some severe attention deficit problems.

"You did a damn fine job on that lightkeeper's cottage," Hector told him as they waited for the women to get ready and the ceremony to begin. He could hear the whole lot of them giggling together through the thin yurt walls, though Tiffany's laugh was so distinct that he could pick it out every time.

"Thanks. I took most of the look from your boat."

"It's a wonderful showpiece, Devin," Gina hugged him then brushed at the lapels of his tuxedo to make sure everything was still in order. "I don't know if I can ever thank you enough."

"I think," he nodded toward the latest burst of giggles, "I'm the one who owes you."

Gina kissed him soundly and Devin supposed that meant they were even.

Trying to avoid blushing, he turned to Hector. "I guess you'll be dropping a permanent anchor in Eagle Cove now."

"Thought I might," Hector nodded, "but my Maggie has other ideas. Said something about retiring and sailing up the Inside Passage, for a start."

"The Dragon is retiring?" He, Gina, Peggy, and both of the judges practically shouted in unison. Tall Guy kept his thoughts to himself.

"Seems she has an idea about training up a new teacher this winter to take over."

"Who?" Again the chorus.

"Well, don't want to spill the beans, but it's seven letters, fifth one is an A…" he stretched out the clue. "And you're about to marry her."

"Huh," was all Devin could manage. Tiffany would be spectacularly good with kids, all kinds. "That's actually a great idea."

Hector nodded, then raised a finger to his lips, "Don't tell. She hasn't approached Tiffany yet."

"Dream on, Hector."

"Okay, don't tell that you heard it from me."

"And who besides you has *your* wife-to-be told this idea to?"

"Aw crap! Caught." His easy shrug earned him sympathetic laughs from around the circle.

There was a sudden squeal of delight from inside the yurt. It sounded terribly un-Tiffany-like, yet he'd never mistake her voice. Perhaps the invitation had just been delivered. The noise level through the walls tripled as it seemed everyone inside was talking at once.

"You know," Peggy appeared to be watching the sky as she spoke. "Speaking of retiring, I'm getting busier than I like with flying and so on. Not getting much time to work on that new airframe I'm restoring."

Devin had learned that nothing would change the path of one of Peggy's thoughts, so he just stayed to the side and waited for when she was good and ready to send the train into the station.

"I was gonna start looking for someone to buy Eagle Cove Contracting…if you happen to know anyone who might be interested. Seasonal work sometimes, but it keeps a soul out of trouble."

Devin rocked back on his heels. That had been one problem he and Tiffany hadn't fully resolved. Her farm wasn't big enough to need two hands very often; actually, with two of them, it rarely took even an hour a day. And though she'd offered, there wasn't a chance in hell he was going to let her give it up and follow him back to Chicago.

He *had* let go of D.R. Builders, but that was always the plan. Originally his father had promised to pay Devin ten million as a "nest egg" when he came aboard at CMC. But if he wasn't joining the family business…he'd haggled his dad up to fifteen, still a bargain. His dad, always shrewd, had taken the deal.

"How much you looking to get for ECC?" He asked Peggy, joining her in watching the sky.

A pair of eagles were soaring far above. Not too near each other, but still together. He'd have to remember to tell Tiffany that it looked like Jake had a girlfriend.

"Well," Peggy now knew the kind of money Devin had and he hoped that she didn't try to gouge him. He wouldn't like it if his or Tiffany's money changed how Eagle Cove treated them.

"We'd have to make a deal," Peggy drawled out and he hoped she was teasing him. Then she looked straight at him and he stopped watching Jake. "First off, you'd have to keep helping me with the hay and the blueberries. The fields and all of the equipment belongs to Becky, but she leases the fields to me because she doesn't care about the hay and lets me borrow the equipment in the deal as long as I keep it all running. I own the grader, but that's long since paid for. Keep my runway level and I'll throw the grader in."

"Seems fair," Devin nodded, trying not to smile. It wasn't the deal you made with an out-of-town sharpie; it was the kind of deal you made with a friend.

"Got all the money I need between the Judge and me, but I could use a hand now and then restoring the new airplane." Which was most of eighty years old.

"Well," Devin loved living in this town, "now that might cost *you*."

Peggy was grinning back at him. This time *she* waited. He was getting the hang of the slower conversations on the Oregon Coast.

"Flying lessons."

"Deal." Peggy held out her hand and they shook on it.

Gina was chatting with Hector and the two judges. Tall Guy was lying down on the job.

And then gentle music came out of a small boom box.

The small crowd quieted.

It was the traditional Bridal Chorus, but played by a solo harp. He'd recognize Tiffany's touch on the strings anywhere.

"Don't screw it up now," Gina whispered to both him and Hector as she positioned them to either side of the altar.

Peggy offered Devin an encouraging slap on the back that was almost hard enough to drive nails—without a hammer.

Jessica, Becky (just starting to bulge at the waist), and Natalya (who hadn't started trying yet, but was "damn well about to") walked out the door and up the short aisle. They were uniformly dressed in little black dresses, like a study in dangerous beauty. Each smiled at him in their own way as they approached. Jessica with the warm hope of a new mother, Becky with a cheery grin, and Natalya still in protective mama bear mode. Once to the front, they sat in the very front row of chairs because Tiffany's deck, *their* deck, wasn't big enough for a large bridal party to be standing.

Then all other thoughts went away.

Tiffany and Maggie Winslow stepped out of the door with Vivian Lamont between them to escort them both down the aisle. Tiffany's mother had also adopted the sexy black dress, but the two brides were dazzling in white. There wasn't a thing schoolmarmish about Maggie Winslow dressed to the hilt.

Devin glanced at his fellow groom, who offered him a happy wink of "Damn but aren't we the lucky ones."

Devin winked back, "No question!"

But if Maggie looked great, Tiffany was dazzling in white satin. Her mother had whisked her away on the jet to some small boutique in Seattle. She'd come back with a wedding dress in an opaque hanging bag labeled "Perrin's Glorious Garb" and a very pleased smile.

It was a simple sheath dress that fit her so perfectly Devin felt as if he was in a dream just looking at her. No longer needing to hide, Tiffany's hair was back in a thick French braid, and that shy smile shown radiant on her lovely face. This was the woman he would happily swear to keep for life. Dragon Winslow—who was looking quite radiant herself—had said it perfectly: Lillian Tiffany Lamont was the true keepsake of Eagle Cove. She would be *his* most precious keepsake forever.

Tall Guy scrambled to his feet and trotted down the aisle to escort his mistress to the altar.

Devin would have to remember to pay him an extra dog biscuit later.

About the Author

M. *L. Buchman has* over 50 novels and 30 short stories in print. His military romantic suspense books have been named Barnes & Noble and NPR "Top 5 of the year" and twice Booklist "Top 10 of the Year," placing two titles on their "Top 101 Romances of the Last 10 Years" list. He has been nominated for the Reviewer's Choice Award for "Top 10 Romantic Suspense of the Year" by RT Book Reviews and was a 2016 RWA RITA finalist. In addition to romance, he also writes thrillers, fantasy, and science fiction.

In among his career as a corporate project manager he has: rebuilt and single-handed a fifty-foot sailboat, both flown and jumped out of airplanes, and designed and built two houses. Somewhere along the way he also bicycled solo around the world.

He is now making his living as a full-time writer on the Oregon Coast with his beloved wife. He is constantly amazed at what you can do with a degree in Geophysics. You may keep up with his writing by subscribing to his newsletter at www. mlbuchman.com.

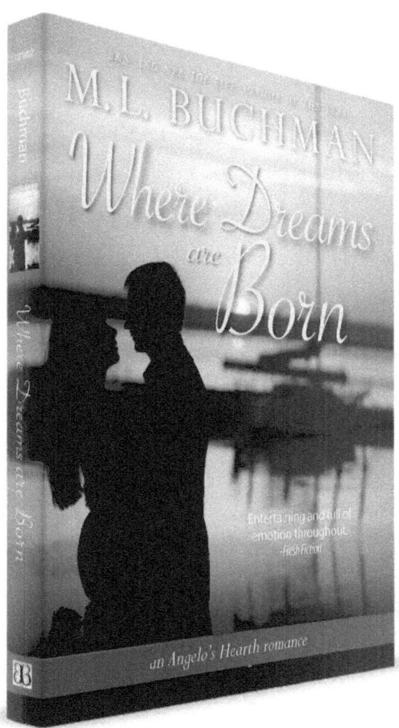

If you enjoyed this series, visit Angelo's Hearth:

Where Dreams Are Born
(excerpt)

Russell locked his studio's door behind the last of the staff, leaned his back against it, and turned off his camera.

He knew it was good. The images were there; he'd really captured them.

But something was missing.

The groove ran so clean when he slid into it.

First his Manhattan high-ceilinged loft would fade into the background, then the strobe lights, reflector umbrellas, and blue and green backdrops all became texture and tone.

Image, camera, and man then became one and they were all that mattered—a single flow of light, beginning before time was counted, and ending its journey in the printed image. One ray of primordial light traveling forever to glisten off the BMW roadster still parked in one corner of the rough-planked wood floor worn smooth by generations of use. Another ray lost in the dark blackness of the finest leather bucket seats. A hundred more picking out the supermodel's perfect hand dangling a single shining and golden key—the image shot just slow enough that the key blurred as it spun, but the logo remained clear.

He couldn't quite put his finger on it…

It would be another great ad by Russell Morgan, Inc. The client would be knocked dead—the ad leaving all others standing still as it roared down the passing lane. This one might get him another Clio, or even a second Mobius.

But…

There wasn't usually a "but."

And there definitely wasn't supposed to be one.

The groove had definitely been there, but he hadn't been in it.

That was the problem. It had slid along, sweeping his staff into their own orchestrated perfection, but he'd remained untouched. That ideal, seamless flow hadn't included him at all.

"Be honest, boyo, that session sucked," he told the empty studio. Everything had come together so perfectly for yet another ad for yet another high-end glossy. *Man, the Magazine* would launch spectacularly in a few weeks, a high-profile mid-December launch, and it would include a never before seen twelve-page spread by the great Russell Morgan. The rag would probably never pay off the lavish launch party of hope, ice sculptures, and chilled magnums of champagne before disappearing like a thousand before it.

He stowed the last camera he'd been using with the others piled by his computer. At the breaker box he shut off the umbrellas, spots, scoops, and washes. The studio shifted from a stark landscape in hard-edged relief to a nest of curious shadows and rounded forms. The tang of hot metal and deodorant were the only lasting result of the day's efforts.

"Morose tonight, aren't we?" he asked his reflection in the darkened window, stories above the streetlights of West 10th. His reflection was wise enough to not answer back. There was never a "down" after a shoot; there was always an "up."

Not tonight.

He'd kept everyone late—even though it was Thanksgiving eve—hoping for that smooth slide of image-camera-man. It was only when he saw the power of the images he captured that he knew he wasn't a part of the chain anymore and decided he'd paid enough triple-time expenses.

The next to last two-page spread was the killer—shot with the door open against a background as black as the sports car's finish. The model's single perfect leg wrapped in thigh-high red-leather boots was all that was visible in the driver's seat. The sensual juxtaposition of woman and sleek machine served as an irresistible focus. It was an ad designed to wrap every person with even a hint of a Y-chromosome around its little finger. And those with only X-chromosomes would simply want to be her. He'd shot a perfect combo of sex for the guys and power for the women.

Even the final one-page image, a close-up of driver's seat from exactly the same angle, revealing not the model but instead a single rose of precisely the same hue as the leather boot, hadn't moved him despite its perfection.

Without him noticing, Russell had become no more than the observer, merely a technician behind the camera. Now that he faced it, months, maybe even a year had passed since he'd been yanked all the way into the light-image-camera-man slipstream. Tonight was a wakeup call and he didn't like it one bit. Wakeup calls were supposed to happen to others, not him. But tonight he could no longer ignore it, he hadn't even trailed in the churned-up wake.

"You're just a creative cog in the advertising machine." Ouch! That one stung, but it didn't turn aside the relentless steamroller of his thoughts speeding down some empty, godforsaken autobahn.

His career was roaring ahead, his business' growth running fast and smooth, but, now that he considered it, he really didn't give a damn.

His life looked perfect, but—"Don't think it!"—his autobahn mind finished despite the command, *it wasn't.*

Russell left his silent reflection to its own thoughts and went through the back door that led to his apartment—closing it tightly on the perfect BMW, the perfect rose, and somewhere, lost among a hundred other props from dozens of other shoots, the long pair of perfect red-leather Chanel boots that had been wrapped around the most expensive legs in Manhattan. He didn't care if he never walked back through that door again. He'd been doing his art by rote; how god-awful sad was that?

And just to rub salt in the wound, he shot *commercial* art.

He'd never had the patience to do art for art's sake. Delayed gratification was his idea of no fun at all. He left the apartment dark with only the city's soft glow through the blind-covered windows revealing the vaguest outlines of the framed art on the wall. Even that almost overwhelmed him tonight.

He didn't want to see the huge prints by the *art* artists: autographed Goldsworthy, Liebowitz, and Joseph Francis' photomosaics for the moderns. A hundred and fifty rare, even one-of-a-kind prints adorned his walls—all the way back through Bourke-White to Russell's prize, an original Daguerre. The Museum of Modern Art kept begging to borrow his collection for a show…and at the moment he was half tempted to dump the whole lot in their Dumpster if they didn't want it.

Crossing the one-room loft apartment—as spacious as the studio—he bypassed the circle of avant garde chairs that were almost as uncomfortable as they looked and avoided the lush black-leather wrap-around sectional sofa of such ludicrous scale that it could be a playpen for two or host a party for twenty. He cracked the fridge in the stainless-steel-and-black corner kitchen searching for something other than his usual beer.

A bottle of Krug.

Maybe he was just being grouchy after a long day's work.

Juice.

No. He'd run his enthusiasm into the ground but good.

Milk even.

Would he miss the camera if he never picked it up again?

No reaction.

Nothing.

Not even a twinge.

That was an emptiness he did not want to face. Especially not alone, in his apartment, in the middle of the world's most vibrant city.

Russell turned away, and just as the door swung closed, the last sliver of light—the relentless chilly blue-white of the refrigerator bulb—shone across his bed. A quick grab snagged the edge of the door and left the narrow beam illuminating a long pale form on his black bedspread.

The Chanel boots weren't in the studio after all. They were still wrapped around those three thousand dollar-an-hour legs: the only clothing on a perfect body, five foot-eleven of intensely toned female anatomy, right down to her exquisitely stair-mastered behind. Her long, white-blond hair lay as a perfect Godiva over her tanned breasts—except for their too exact symmetry, even the closest inspection didn't reveal the work done there. She lay with one leg raised just ever so slightly to hide what was meant to be revealed later.

Melanie.

By the steady rise and fall of her flat stomach, he knew she'd fallen asleep while waiting for him to finish in the studio.

How long had they been an item? Two months? Three?

She'd made him feel alive…at least when he was actually with her. Melanie was the supermodel in his bed or on his arm at yet another SoHo gallery opening. Together they journeyed to sharp parties and trendy three-star restaurants where she dazzled and wooed yet another gathering of New York's finest with her ever so soft, so sensual, and so studied French accent. Together they were wired into the heart of the in-crowd.

But that wasn't him, was it? It didn't sound like the Russell he once knew.

Perhaps "they" were about how *he* looked on *her* arm?

Did she know tomorrow was the annual Thanksgiving ordeal at his parents? The grand holiday gathering that he'd rather die than attend? Any number of eligible woman would be floating about his parents' house out in Greenwich; anyone able to finagle an invitation would attend in hopes of snaring one of *People Magazine's* "100 Most Eligible." They all wanted to land the heir to a billion or some such; though he was wealthy enough on his own, by his own sweat, to draw anyone's attention. He ranked number twenty-four on the list this year—up from forty-seven the year before despite Tom Cruise being available yet again.

But not Melanie. He knew that it wasn't the money that drew her. Yes, she wanted him. But even more, she wanted the life that came with him—wrapped in the man-package. She wanted The Life. The one that *People Magazine* readers dreamed about between glossy pages.

His fingertips were growing cold where they held the refrigerator door cracked open.

If he woke her there'd be amazing sex. Or a great party to go to. Or…

Did he want "Or"? What more did he want from her?

Sex. Companionship. An energy, a vivacity, a thirst he feared that he lacked. Yes.

But where was that smooth synchronicity hiding, like the light-image-camera-man of photography that he'd lost? Where lurked that perfect flow from one person to another? Did she feel it? Could he ever feel it?

"More?" he whispered into the darkness to test the sound.

The refrigerator door slid shut—escaping from his numbed fingers—which plunged the apartment back into darkness, taking Melanie along with it.

His breath echoed in the vast darkness. Proof that he was alive, if nothing more.

It was time to close the studio—time to be done with Russell Incorporated.

Then what?

Maybe Angelo would know what to do. He always claimed that he did. Maybe this time Russell would actually listen to his almost-brother, though he knew from the experience of being himself for the last thirty years that was unlikely.

Seattle.

Damn! He'd have to go to bloody Seattle to find his best friend. There was a possible upside to such a trip—maybe there'd be a flight out before tomorrow's mess at his parents'. He slapped his pocket, but once again he'd set his phone down in some unknown corner of the studio and it would take forever to find. He really needed two—one chained down so that he could always find it to call the other.

Russell considered the darkness. He could guarantee that Seattle wouldn't be a big hit with Melanie.

Now if he only knew whether that was a good thing or bad.

\# \# \#

"If you were still alive, you'd pay for this one, Daddy." The moment the words escaped her lips, Cassidy Knowles slapped a hand over her mouth to negate them, but it was too late.

The sharp wind took her words and threw them back into the pines, guilt and all. It might have stopped her, if it didn't make this the hundredth time she'd cursed him this morning.

She leaned in and forged her way downhill until the muddy path broke free from the mossy smell of the forest. Her Stuart Weitzman boots were long since soaked through, and now her feet were freezing. In a last gasp effort before the chill trees would let her go, a root snagged two-inch heels again and tried to flip her into the mud.

Free at last, Cassidy stared at the lighthouse. It perched upon a point of rock: tall and white, with its red roof as straight and snug as a prim bonnet. A narrow trail traced along the top of the breakwater leading to the lighthouse. The parking lot, much to her chagrin, was empty; six, beautiful, empty spaces.

"Sorry, ma'am," park rangers were always polite when telling you what you couldn't do. "The parking lot by the light is for physically-challenged visitors only. You'll have to park here. It *is* just a short walk to the lighthouse."

The fact that she was dressed for an afternoon lunch at Pike Place Market safe in Seattle's downtown rather than a blustery mile-long trek on the first day of the year didn't phase the ranger in the slightest.

Cassidy should have gone home, would have if it hadn't been for the letter stuffed deep in her pocket. So, instead of a tasty treat in a cozy deli, she'd buttoned the top button of her suede Bernardo jacket and headed out onto the trail. At least the promised rain had yet to arrive, so the jacket was only cold, not wet.

Finally free of the trees, a new problem arose. Beyond the lighthouse ranged a vast expanse of Puget Sound and it was being whipped into a frenzy like someone desperate to make a towering meringue rather than a smooth zabaglione custard. Whitecaps tore off the tops of waves, dark clouds scudded low over the water, and the far shore might as well have been the North Pole rather than Bainbridge Island for how inviting it looked. The towering heights of the Olympic Mountains scraped at the clouds with glacier-clad peaks.

Her jacket's stylish cut had never been intended to fight off these bajillion mile-an-hour gusts that snapped it painfully against her hips. Her black leggings ranged about five layers short of tolerable and a far, far cry from warm.

Approaching the lighthouse across the exposed—and utterly vacant—parking lot, any part of her that had been merely numb slipped right over to quick frozen. Leaning into the wind to stay upright, tears streaming from her eyes, she could think of a thing or two to tell her father despite his recent demise and her general feelings about the usefulness of upbraiding a dead man.

"What a stupid present!" Her shout was torn word-by-word, syllable-by-syllable and sent flying back toward her nice warm car and the ever-so-polite park ranger.

A calendar. Her dad had given her a stupid calendar of stupid lighthouses and a stupid letter to open at each stupid one. He'd been very insistent, made her promise. One she couldn't ignore. A deathbed promise.

Cassidy leaned grimly forward to walk through the onslaught only to have the wind abruptly cease. She staggered, nearly planting her face on the pavement before another gust rescued her but sent her crabbing sideways. With resolute force, she planted one foot in front of the other until she'd crossed the open pavement. There weren't any handicapped people crazy enough to come here New Year's morning. No people at all for that matter.

The empty lot and the lighthouse were separated by a short path along the top of a rocky breakwater. Boulders the size of her car had been piled up to resist the pounding of the sea. The top had been made into a solid path, so her footing was sure even if the wind continued to buffet her wildly.

The building's wall was concrete, worn smooth by a thousand storms and a hundred coats of brilliant white paint. With the wind practically pinning her to the outside of the building, she peeked into one of the windows. Her hair blew about so that it beat on her eyes and mouth trying to simultaneously blind and choke her. With one hand, she smashed the unruly mass mostly to one side. With the other she shaded the dusty window.

The cobwebbed glass revealed an equally unkempt interior: no lightkeeper sitting in his rocking chair before a merry fire with his smoking pipe and a lighthouse cat curled in his lap. There was some sort of a rusty engine not attached to anything. A bucket of old tools. A couple of paint cans.

A high wave crashed into the rocks with a thundering shudder that ran up through the heels of her boots and whipped a chill spray into the wind. Salt water on suede—Daddy now owed her a new coat as well.

Cassidy edged along the foundation until she found a calmer spot, a little windshadow behind the lighthouse where the wind chill ranked merely miserable rather than horrific on the suck-o-meter. Squatting down behind one of the breakwater's boulders helped a tiny bit more. She peeled off her thin leather gloves and blew against her fingertips to warm them enough so that they'd work. Once she'd regained some modicum of feeling, she pulled out the letter.

She couldn't feel his actual writing, though she ran her fingertips over it again and again. His Christmas present: a five-dollar calendar of Washington lighthouses from the hospital gift store and a dozen thin envelopes wrapped in a old x-ray folder with no ribbon, no paper.

In the end he'd foiled her final Christmas hunt. It had been her great yearly quest—the ultimate grail of childhood—finding the key present before Christmas morning. There was no present he could hide that she couldn't find. Not the Cabbage Patch Kid when she was six; the one she'd had to hold with her arm in a cast after falling off the kitchen stool she'd dragged into her father's closet to aid the search. Not the used VW Rabbit he'd hidden out in the wine shed thinking that she never went there anymore. And she didn't, except for some reason that day before her eighteenth Christmas.

A part of her wanted to crumple the letter up and throw it into the sea. It was too soon. She didn't want to face the pain again.

Too soon.

She looked out at the crashing waves. With a sudden howl of wind, a slash of spray roared by mere feet from her face, barely averted by the staunch tower of the lighthouse. Clearly someone wasn't happy about her desire to avoid the task at hand.

The rest of her body did what it supposed to do. The dutiful daughter opened the envelope and pinned the letter against her thigh so that she could read the slashing scrawl that was her father's. Even as weak with sickness as he must have been, it looked scribed in stone. His bold-stroke writing gave the words a force and strength just as his deep voice had once sounded strong enough to keep the world at bay for a little girl.

Dearest Ice Sweet,

Available soon at fine retailers everywhere.

Other works by M. L. Buchman:

Angelo's Hearth
Where Dreams are Born
Where Dreams Reside
Maria's Christmas Table
Where Dreams Unfold
Where Dreams Are Written

Eagle Cove
Return to Eagle Cove
Recipe for Eagle Cove
Longing for Eagle Cove
Keepsake for Eagle Cove

The Night Stalkers
MAIN FLIGHT
The Night Is Mine
I Own the Dawn
Wait Until Dark
Take Over at Midnight
Light Up the Night
Bring On the Dusk
By Break of Day
WHITE HOUSE HOLIDAY
Daniel's Christmas
Frank's Independence Day
Peter's Christmas
Zachary's Christmas
Roy's Independence Day
AND THE NAVY
Christmas at Steel Beach
Christmas at Peleliu Cove

5E
Target of the Heart
Target Lock on Love

Firehawks
MAIN FLIGHT
Pure Heat
Full Blaze
Hot Point
Flash of Fire
SMOKEJUMPERS
Wildfire at Dawn
Wildfire at Larch Creek
Wildfire on the Skagit

Delta Force
Target Engaged
Heart Strike

Deities Anonymous
Cookbook from Hell: Reheated
Saviors 101

Dead Chef Thrillers
Swap Out!
One Chef!
Two Chef!

SF/F Titles
Nara
Monk's Maze
The Me and Elsie Chronicles

www.ingramcontent.com/pod-product-compliance
Lightning Source LLC
Chambersburg PA
CBHW060553190726
48283CB00003B/992